Crossroads Soulmates

Misty D Tackett

This work of fiction contains a partial memoir with authentic depictions of persons, living and deceased, events, and dates. The names have been changed to protect their identities. Fictional characters by name and description similar to those living or deceased are coincidental and not intended by the author.

ISBN: 978-1-7373249-7-3

Cover designed by: Misty D. Tacket in Canva Create

Printed in the United States of America

DEDICATION

For my soulmate
Thank you for weathering the journey through life by my side.
I love you, my husband.

CONTENTS

"I am my beloved's and my beloved is mine."

Song of Solomon 8:3

PROLOG

In times of war, humanity has risen with a conviction born from great passion. We arm ourselves for battle with a steadfast heart and righteous intent. We stand in opposition to fear which rises from pride.

Pride is a self-appointed statute in which we lean on our own understanding. And by any means, through rise or fall, pride can taint our convictions. It can create a cause in which we wear a crown of doubt, align ourselves with the opposition, and set ourselves up for persecution.

Pride kills in many ways and by any means, and it will not acknowledge its flawed convictions. And when we finally fall victim to its transgressions, we are left questioning if any good will come.

Can redemption break the chains that hold us captive?

I wondered what penance I would pay for my transgressions. The self-sabotaging, loathing thoughts in my head from which I longed to be free caused me to reel in a downward spiral of depression.

I had long dreamt of being someone else, living another life. I knew it was selfish and illogical. My husband loved me, and I loved him. We had a whirlwind romance, made a life, and had three beautiful children together. I loved and cherished them, but my heart constantly ached because I could never love myself, no matter how much I tried.

I felt trapped inside an aching, ever-aging body. I longed to look and feel young and beautiful again. I wanted adventures like the ones I read and wrote about in grand romances. There within those pages, the characters had one ultimate truth. They held firm to their convictions to pull them through the storm. And it was unique to their individual story.

One ultimate truth was that if we followed our hearts, all roads would lead home. After all, home is where the heart is. But what happens when one's heart feels stranded at a crossroads?

I lacked the courage of my convictions to decide which way to go because I leaned too long on my own understanding. And my strength had long ago depleted.

So, the heavens took up a cause to intervene, and at the end of my life, a wonderful life I had taken for granted, I stood inexplicably at a crossroads.

I died.

But I did not arrive at my hopeful destination.

ALPHA

A warm draft blew in from an open window in the dark hallway, where to my right, a dim flame from a lantern cast shadows on the opposing wall. I shifted on my feet, and the wooden floorboards creaked. I didn't know where I was as I looked around and took note of the dark forest green shiplap walls with the paint cracked and worn in a few places.

Cigar smoke wafted up the staircase before me, and the sounds of life rose in my ears like someone slowly turned up the volume. It sounded like a party happening downstairs. People were singing, cheering, laughing. Corks popped, glasses clinked, and music played. Beyond the window, the celebration continued out onto the streets. Car horns were honking, voices were cheering, and firecrackers were going off. I recoiled when I heard a few gunshots. Worried someone was out there on some killing spree, I crouched low on the floor, only releasing a breath of relief when I heard voices cheering joyously.

Frozen in place and not knowing which way to go, I felt like I was waking up for the first time. Where was I? I tried to get a grip on my unfamiliar surroundings when suddenly I heard a door open and close and footsteps coming up the dark stairs. I didn't know if I was in danger when a tall, dark figure appeared and halted at the top.

I felt their eyes on me, though I could not distinguish their hidden features in shadow. They seemed to be assessing me as my pounding heart rose in my throat and assaulted my ears. I swallowed nervously, wondering if death was standing before me.

But then they spoke, and the deep male voice sounded warm and alluring.

"You are a beautiful woman."

Was he talking to me?

Undoubtedly, the man was talking to someone else. I looked around and behind myself to see who he was talking to, but no one else was there. He stepped into the dim light, and his features were alarming.

Why would someone who looks like him tell me I'm beautiful? I'm not beautiful.

In my late forties, my hair was mostly silver. My face was thick with a double chin. My eyelids drooped, and my nose sat prominently on my face above thin lips. My stomach protruded beyond my meager breasts, my thick and flabby thighs jiggled with unsightly cellulite, my hips were too broad, and my rear end abundant. I did not fit any description of beauty in my perception. I looked and felt old, depleted of energy, and gravely depreciated in what nice looks I may have had long ago. Yet my husband still loved me. For the life of me, I couldn't understand why he did. I felt so disgusted with myself. I scarcely allowed him to love me in any intimate fashion.

Too often, I had pushed him away. I felt so guilty for doing that to him. He was a good man, a wonderful husband. He deserved better.

And here, this man who looked like he belonged with a barrage of beauties fawning over him stood before me, looking at me like I was the only woman in the world. He was the epitome of tall, dark, and handsome. He had such adoration in his eyes. He reached out with his hand toward my face, his fingers curled toward his palm, ready to caress my cheek with his knuckles.

I jerked back.

"I'm looking for my husband," I said with a clipped tone.

He paused, lowering his hand, his lips curving upward, set into a masculine jawline. He had a face that looked like Michelangelo himself had sculpted. His eyes, indecipherable in color due to his dilated pupils in the dim light, captured the reflection of the glowing flame.

"My apologies. Mrs. Akner, wife of Sergeant Akner? Correct?" He looked at me as if I were playing a game with him, even going so far as to wink at me.

"Mrs. Akner? No, I'm," before I could finish, he cut me off.

"Follow me, ma'am."

He slipped past me in the narrow hallway, and I instinctively turned sideways, sucking in my gut to give him room to pass. He headed away from the stairs where the party continued on the floor below. The music sounded like a genre of a bygone era. The murmuring voices below were unrecognizable. I didn't know what the celebration was about, and everything around me felt like an echo—an echo from the past.

How did I end up here?

My body felt on autopilot as I turned to follow the man; my high-heeled shoes clicked on the floorboards. The swish of my knee-length dress rubbed across my thighs.

Wait! I never wore heels! And why am I wearing a dress? I hated wearing dresses.

But then I realized my right hip didn't hurt as I moved, and I no longer limped or hobbled. My body felt light, graceful, and fluid, much like I thought a dancer would. In my confusion and lack of concern about this stranger's intentions, I was more confused about the feel of my body. For some strange reason, my head ached. I touched the side of it and winced.

He didn't seem to notice as he opened the door, struck a match, and lit another lantern; the glow emanated around his tall frame. He turned, held the lantern before him, and like a gentleman, gestured for me to enter the room. I glimpsed his handsome face as I passed through the threshold and entered a bedroom.

Further confused, I turned to look at him. He wore a devilishly handsome smile as he said, "Well, you found him. Aren't you going to welcome your husband home from the war, Mrs. Akner?"

"Why are you call-," I paused. Something didn't feel right. Was this a joke?

He approached me, and his hand grazed down my arm seductively. It triggered a knee-jerk reaction as my body jumped, combined with a surprised intake of air filling my lungs. My entire physicality tingled, and he released a deep enchanting laugh at my response. He seemed so self-assured and somewhat cocky as if he'd captured something no other man had obtained.

Uncertainty within me grew, and I shifted farther away from the man as he closed the door. He turned the lock, and my breathing escalated. What did he want from me? *Me?*

He turned back toward me, loosening his necktie and undoing his shirt's top buttons while drinking in my face and body with a smoldering expression. I backed away, looking left and right for an escape when my backside collided with a metal bedframe. I reached behind and grasped the scrolling cold iron. My heart started to pound frantically in my chest. Why did I follow him? Why didn't my flight instincts kick in?

"Well?" His brow furrowed, followed by a look of anticipation and longing.

I swallowed the knot in my throat, "Well, what?"

Heat stirred in my belly. What the Hell was wrong with me?

Good grief! He was so devastatingly handsome. He looked somewhat like my husband, albeit taller. His body was solid and youthful. His dark hair was thick with slight waves on top and trimmed close on the sides in a militant fashion. I could finally make out the color of his eyes, a striking blue. The longer he held my gaze, the more he reminded me of my husband.

Where was my husband? He said he was going to take me to him. Didn't he?

The closer this man stepped to me, the farther away I felt from my life. *My life? Was this my life?*

He stood so close to me, and I suddenly felt like I belonged here with him. This place and time felt like it had some relatable meaning I could connect with.

As I took in the details of his outfit and realized he was wearing a World War II Army uniform, something in my subconscious snapped. My husband was obsessed with World War II. He enjoyed collecting memorabilia, watching documentaries and movies, and reading almost every book. A few times, he confessed to me; he felt he was born in the wrong era and should have been there fighting on the front lines. Maybe he had. Perhaps he felt an attachment to some small glimmer of a past life.

I didn't know if reincarnation was real or not. Some people believed, and some didn't. I did learn a thing or two about being born again as a Christian woman. I still struggled to see or love myself the way God did, and it was a never-ending internal battle with my mental illness.

After my mother died three years ago, I slept too much of my life away. I did it to escape reality and to dream. My dreams were so vivid. It must be what was happening to me. I was sleeping, and my mind was spinning another elaborate tale of sensual desire and intimidation. Deep down, I desired to be with my husband in the sweet intimacy we once shared in our youth.

The man's alluring voice questioned a name, "Nora?"

"I, I'm not," I stammered. My muscles locked as he grasped my shoulders, his eyes holding my own; the handsome soldier pulled me closer.

Too close! I panicked.

Energy rushed through me like when I fell in love with my husband twenty-eight years ago. It was that combination of dreamy desire and a deep unquenchable longing for physical connection.

"You're not what?" he asked with a cheeky grin.

His scent of spicey, clean aftershave clung to my nose. It was heady. Intoxicating. It reminded me of the first time my husband shaved off his mustache, which sparked a desire to get physically acquainted.

I tried to pull away from the stranger before me, but there was nowhere to go. I had a feeling if I rejected him, he might collapse from a broken heart. Whomever he thought I was, he was undeniably infatuated. My heart began to warm. At the same time, my brain screamed, *Stop!! You've never been unfaithful to your husband, and you won't start now!*

I blinked, and my mouth opened to protest his advances. Before the words left my lips, he cut me off again.

"Nora, I understand you're nervous. We just married before I left, and we barely knew each other. But I feel like I've gotten to know you through our written exchanges. I have all the letters you wrote. Reading them helped get me through it all. I've been waiting for this moment to be back in your arms. Ever since we parted, I felt so guilty for leaving you behind. Every battle I faced was one moment closer to winning this war and returning home to you."

***

Blindsided by a flashback, I sat beside my husband, watching historical footage of soldiers storming the beaches of Normandy, survival in the trenches as artillery rained down, the bombing of Hiroshima, airplanes roaring through the sky, gunning at one another, M1 tanks tearing across the European countryside, and submarine-launched missiles attacking naval fleets. Behind it all, members of the Great Generation sat in interviews, describing their personal experiences. Newspaper headlines declared WAR END—flashes of people celebrating in the streets. *Operation Magic Carpet* was in full effect, and we were *'Alive In '45'*.

"The war," I whispered.

He flinched at the sound of firecrackers popping outside the window, and suddenly I saw the vulnerability in his eyes. I knew what this reaction was. Post Traumatic Stress Disorder. Let There Be Light, produced in 1946, would acknowledge and highlight the disorder. Many soldiers would go on to suffer from this affliction, taking a toll on their lives to the point of ending their suffering by desperate means.

It was then that my heart went out to this stranger. I pressed my hand to his cheek and looked at him empathetically. I wanted to pray for him, but he looked at me strangely.

"Nora. Why are you looking at me that way? I'm home. We're safe now. We can start our life together. At last."

At first, I shook my head and then nodded. "My husband," I began to say. His fingers gently grasped and tugged at my chin, and I lifted my eyes to meet his hooded gaze.

"Yes, Nora. I am your husband, Roderick Gregory Akner. We met at the diner down on Monmouth Street two years ago. Remember?" A charming yet teasing smile stretched his very kissable lips. Something akin to a spiritual light flashed in his eyes.

Was seeing believing? Because I thought I had just caught a glimpse of my husband's soul, and I couldn't believe it. His words echoed in my mind.

"I always felt like I was born in the wrong era. I should have been a soldier in World War II."

"Once a soldier," I said aloud.

"Always a soldier," Roderick finished. He chuckled and pulled me into a tight embrace. His heart was drumming loudly inside his chest. I tentatively moved my arms around him. My fingers intertwined, and my hands rested at the nap of his neck. With a ragged breath, I released the pent-up tension I had held in, and everything felt. Right.

"Gregory," I began to say. That was my husband's first name. *In another life*, I thought to myself.

"My middle name? Well, I suppose if that's what you want to call me, I'm okay with that." With an amused exhale, his warm breath hit the shell of my ear, and tears pricked at the corners of my eyes.

Why did Roderick have to be so kind, warm, and funny? Just like my Gregory. He felt so familiar. I'd often felt like we were soul mates and wondered if we had met in another life. Roderick called me Nora, and I realized there was so much more that I needed to learn about myself.

"The letters," I said.

"You kept the ones I sent to you?" My husband asked.

My Husband.

I nodded, though I wasn't entirely sure. I didn't know this identity. My mind felt detached from this body I was in, but, like any devoted wife awaiting her husband's return from war, Nora would have kept and treasured every written word. I didn't know where on Earth Nora had put Roderick's letters.

"I'm sorry I didn't write to you as much. I…." I halted Roderick's words with my fingers pressed to his lips.

"It's okay. I understand. More than you know," I replied.

In 1997, fifty-two years ahead, my husband, Gregory, was deployed on a peacekeeping mission to Bosnia. We had been married for nearly two years, and being separated by an ocean and seven months almost killed me. My depression hit hard as I sat alone in our home, feeling like half of me was missing—

my *soul mate.*

Roderick nodded and said, "I know you do. I felt like part of my soul had left me. Being away from you for so long nearly broke me. Do you understand?"

His words felt like a gust had knocked me over. I nodded vigorously and began to sob. I felt the sadness stretch over the decades in reverse, from the future to the past. It slammed into me so hard it made my chest ache. He held me tight as my tears soaked his shirt, and my nose became stuffy.

"Oh, Nora."

The name resounded through his chest, where my ear rested against his beating heart. I wanted to tell him *my* name. That I am Racheal, and he is Gregory. We've been married for twenty-eight years and had three beautiful children together. We built a beautiful life. One that I had taken for granted. I allowed myself to wither away, not caring about myself enough to reclaim that beauty. We had our problems, our ups, and downs, but it didn't matter to everything else in comparison. He always loved me through thick and thin, and I was too selfish to let go of the loathing I carried on my shoulders, the way I despised myself more than I loved him and our children. It was soul-crushing. I wanted to tell him how sorry I was. But the man standing before me would not understand what I was saying.

Instead, Roderick Gregory Akner, husband of Nora, asked me a question that made my heart skip a beat.

"May I kiss my beautiful bride?"

Suddenly, drawn back, or should I say forward, to a particular memory where I sat on the bathtub ledge, I watched in fascination as each razor stroke erased facial hair above Gregory's upper lip. When he finished, I stood looking at his reflection in the mirror.

"You look so much younger without it."

"Want to kiss me and see what it feels like?" He smiled devilishly.

He was so irresistible. I put my arms around him, pressing my lips to his. Silky smooth skin replaced the scruffy hair that used to scrape against my mouth and face. The new sensation and crisp, clean scent of shaving cream made me giddy.

"Oooh! I feel like I'm kissing another man." I swooned. "It feels so naughty. Mmm, you look and feel so sexy!"

"I'm okay with naughty." Gregory grinned. "Besides, I'm your husband's evil twin, and you've been with me before." He snickered deviously, and I laughed.

Gregory had a way of stirring a fire in me with his upbeat sense of humor. The evil twin was our inside joke when he was on the prowl. Supposedly, his evil twin had stolen my virginity in his single soldier studio apartment to the song Eternal Flame.

"Oh yeah," I acknowledged, "And I'm Cindy."

My husband laughed. Cindy was the name some of his fellow soldier friends used when I showed up at military family gatherings. It was one of those long-running inside jokes that had only slightly offended me initially. Still, I later adopted and adapted it as ammunition to face off with the offenders.

Life felt so carefree back then.

"Nora?" Roderick's voice pulled me back.

I blinked and saw his concern.

"Where did you go?" he asked.

I smiled and replied, "I had a vision. Of the future."

"Hope I was in it," Roderick jested.

I felt as giddy at this moment as I had felt then. A giggle erupted from my mouth. "Yes," I replied with flirtatious laughter.

My husband smiled. "What was it about?"

"This!" I pressed my lips to his mouth, and it felt like that moment. Naughty, like I was kissing another man, because at this moment, in a way, I was. A euphoric sensation rushed through my body. I was tingling from head to toe. We were young and in love again. It was new, yet old, in the past and the present.

Then came a snag, and my train of thought shifted. I thought about our future life together and mourned for the children we were yet to have. I knew who they were, their appearance, and their unique personalities. From their conception to the moment they were born, Gregory and I watched them grow from rolling around inside my womb, to birth, to adorable infants, toddlers, preteens, teenagers, and beautiful young adults. And here, I had left them behind. The guilt tugged at me.

A chasm seized my chest, and I broke the kiss—the kiss I wanted to share with my husband and more. The initial desire came rushing back with a tsunami-like force. I wanted to make our life together again and live each moment the same, all the ups and downs, like a rattling, raging rollercoaster, lifting to emotional heights and plunging to the depths of despair, making our way in a rush through time and twisting our world upside down. I wanted the good, the bad, the ugly, the beautiful.

Damned, the enemy to Hell!

Every life occurrence which had broken me had also made me. It was God's intention. *You are beautiful, my daughter. I gave you a beautiful life. Can't you see that?*

I wanted to wake up. I wanted so badly to come back to the future present. My life is my adventure. My husband and our family is my heart and soul's desire.

The life we built mattered.

All of it!

BRAVO

I saw myself lying in a hospital bed. My husband and our youngest daughter, Sarah, were at my bedside crying as a heart monitor beeped signs of life. I was still here, still clinging, still holding on. I tried to open my eyes and could see my chest rising and falling with each breath I took. I felt my baby girl's delicate hand wrapped around my own. She sniffed, with the sound of tears clogging her throat.

Don't cry, baby girl. I tried to say, but my lips would not move.

My head began to ache again, my soul pulled backward, and it felt like I was riding a subway train at light speed in reverse. I opened my eyes, and I was back in Roderick's arms. I wanted to stay, but I wanted to go. I couldn't make up my mind.

How would our lives pan out together? It was clear we loved one another. Deeply so. Curiosity pulled at my mind. Was I to live a replay of my past life with my husband before he became my husband again?

"You left me again." Roderick looked at me worriedly.

"I'm sorry. I don't know what's happening to me," I stated honestly. How could I explain it?

My husband looked at me, so hopeful. I was at a *crossroads*. I remembered the first time I'd felt this way.

***

I had asked God to bring me, my life partner, three months before Gregory and I met. I was specific about how he would look, his personality, his ethics, and that he shared the same Christian faith my father, *a World War II soldier*, instilled in me. God delivered. But the devil was an interloper who enjoyed planting seeds of doubt.

We all have pasts. Gregory and I had been dating for three weeks when he told me everything about his life, including all his mistakes. Gregory realized he needed to change and asked God's forgiveness. My heart was drawn even more to him with that admission.

I answered a phone call at my job from a woman who said she knew Gregory. She gave details of his past, claiming that she only looked out for my young, tender heart. I went along with the pretense of not knowing who she was. But I knew! I allowed her to tell me everything, politely thanked her for her courtesy, and ended the call.

I knew her motives were to break Gregory and me apart. The information she so willingly provided did not deter my feelings for him. My only concern was that she might be a constant festering wound that would continue to re-open. I did not want to deal with any drama in any relationship.

As clear as a cloudless spring day, Gregory arrived at my door to whisk me away for the weekend. He stood on the front porch looking fresh and leisurely in his red jogging suit. His big smile changed into a frown at seeing the look on my face. My arms were folded across my chest, angry that she had tried to get under my skin.

"What's wrong?" he asked.

"I got a phone call at work yesterday. Someone from your past was trying to make it sound like you are a bad person, but they didn't tell me anything new."

"Oh." Gregory looked down solemnly.

I could see the heavy emotion hanging, teetering on the ledge. What I said next determined whether two hearts destined for one another would break or combine and become stronger. I already knew what my heart wanted, but I could still see the *crossroads* we faced as we looked each other in the eye.

"If you want me to leave, I'll understand." He looked on the verge of tears. And dammit, if my heart didn't shatter at the sight of his impending emotional collapse. I couldn't do that to him. I couldn't do it to me, and I couldn't do it to us! Because I envisioned a future for us together.

"No," I said quickly. "But I need to know if she will continue to be a problem that won't go away. I know what she wants. Well, guess what? I know better. And I may live in a cake eater town, but I wasn't born and raised here."

Gregory laughed, and hope shone in his glassy eyes that had been on the verge of shedding. "She won't be a problem. I already made it clear to her that we were through, and I was moving on with my life, and she needed to do the same. She played and strung me along, and I'm tired of games. Since meeting you, you're all I think about. I want what we have, and what we have is something real. I'm in love with you, Rachael."

Tears slipped from my eyes. "I'm in love with you too, Gregory."

***

"I'm still in love with you, Nora," Roderick confessed. I looked at Roderick standing before me. He was holding my hands in his. I was still here.

"You seem lost," he said.

"I can't lie to you, Roderick. I am feeling a little bit lost." If he only knew why.

"Memory lane, or road to the future?" His inquisitive expression made my chest squeeze with anxiety. Something I knew well.

"I little bit of both. But both include you. I do love you. My husband."

Roderick smiled brightly. "Well, I guess we'll navigate it together. Are you ready?"

I nodded. "Uhm, Yeeeah?" It came out as an apprehensive drawl.

I mean, I was ready, but still, these different bodies, our present bodies, felt so foreign. How did I navigate the course of expectancy and intimacy between us when we were different people?

Quite literally!

"It's okay if you're not ready, darling. I won't push you. This is new for both of us, and we are a team. But," Roderick paused, drawing a deep breath from the oxygen surrounding us, and his body quivered, "I'm dying to get to know you better. In so many beautiful ways."

My husband winked, and I released a nervous laugh. A timid vulnerability, a tender aching like the first time we made love, had me trembling. The anticipation was exciting and scary. Somewhere inside, it still felt like my actions would betray my beliefs.

Till death do us part.

Those words rang like an earsplitting gong. I was mindful of this moment, yet still aware that I drew breath in my future life. It was a paradoxical conundrum that left my mind spinning.

The naughty temptress on my shoulder had always wanted an experience like this. I had never known such an experience with another man. Gregory had been my one and only, and I was somewhat curious about Roderick's abilities and attributes. But, not only that. As my curiosity grew, I became increasingly aware of my current body, desiring to know what Nora looked like.

"Do you mind if I go freshen up?" I asked Roderick.

"Darling, you're already a breath of fresh air. There's not a thing I would mind in getting to know your beautiful body better."

Whoo-wee! My husband was a smooth talker. I bit my lips to maintain control of my nerves. I needed an excuse to see what he saw when he looked at me.

"I *do* need the bathroom," I stated. Roderick turned and walked to the door. He unlocked and opened it, pointing to the next door on the left.

"Here. Take this with you." He handed me the lantern. "Hopefully, the lights will come back on soon. But I must admit, this light creates quite the romantic ambiance."

I smiled as I took the lantern's handle, and goosebumps sprung along my flesh when our fingers brushed. I pushed the bathroom door open.

"Sure, you don't want me to join you, Mrs. Akner?" I could hear that mischievous smile in his voice. I laughed because that was something Gregory would often say.

I couldn't use more modern terminology to deter him, like, '*I have to blow up the bathroom, drop a stink bomb*,' or other such nonsense. I knew he wouldn't understand the crude reference.

Instead, I replied, "I just need a moment."

"Take as long as you need. Just not all night." Roderick grinned. The door creaked as I slowly closed it between us. Roderick watched me the whole time as if I might disappear forever.

Maybe I would. I didn't know. I held the lantern before me and saw the mirror above the porcelain sink. Approaching cautiously, I set the lantern down, keeping my eyes downcast, as I prepared myself mentally for whom I would see looking back. I shut my eyes tight and raised my head.

"Okay, Rachael. In one, two, three." My lids opened, and I had to blink away the blurriness from the tears I had shed. The first thing I noticed was Nora's surprised expression. I was a version of my younger future self. Only this me had a lovely slender face with green eyes, thick lashes, rosy lips, and a pert nose. My hair was strawberry blonde and styled in finger-rolled curls with bobby pins holding it in place. I took a few steps back and observed the body I'd always dreamed of having.

I looked like a dancer, a slender ballerina, to be more precise, though my breasts were fuller and more symmetrical. I filled out my dress nicely with my curves in all the right places. My dress looked handmade, and looking down at my pinpricked, chipped fingernails, I felt I may have made the dress myself.

Not too shabby!

I wasn't an exquisite beauty, but I passed for moderately attractive. My chin had a small scar, and my ears looked a bit large compared to my slender face. I smiled at my reflection and felt ridiculous. Even though this body was Nora's, I was critiquing my appearance as I noticed the mascara streaks running down my cheeks. My reddish rose-stained lips had slightly smeared from the kiss Roderick and I shared.

I found a washcloth, ran it under the water tap, and cleaned my face. Removing all my makeup, I could see my natural rosy complexion. I noted minor blemishes on my face but dismissed them as most of my skin looked like radiant porcelain youth. I looked to be somewhere in my early twenties; I wagered a guess.

I checked my breath, which was fine, and ran my hands down my arms, legs, and waist, noting my well-toned musculature. I must have done palates on the daily. I only had the slightest pouch on my lower belly.

I undid the side zipper of my dress and shrugged my arms and shoulders free, letting it slip down to my waist, where I held it. The bra felt more like a torture device beneath my silky white lace-trimmed slip, so I let my dress fall, removed the offending undergarment, and sighed in relief. I stared at myself a few minutes longer, aware that Roderick was waiting for me in the next room. My fingernails went to my mouth, and I began chewing on them in a nervous fit. Was I still a virgin? Women were more reserved in the 1940s. Right?

I giggled like a loon. *In the 40s!!! I was in my 40s, living in the 20s next century over! This whole situation must be some cosmic joke.*

I had no idea if Roderick and Nora had consummated their marriage before he left for the war. I wondered how impromptu their nuptials had been. I felt shy all of a sudden. A knock sounded at the door, and I jumped.

"Are you all right in there?" Roderick asked. I nodded, then face-palmed my forehead, realizing he could not see me.

"Uhm. Yeah, I'm fine. Be out in a moment." I waited till I heard Roderick's footsteps retreat.

When he closed the bedroom door, I looked at myself in the mirror, deciding to give myself a small pep talk.

"Okay, Racheal. You are Nora! And even though Nora may not know crap, you've done this before. He's your husband, and you love each other. You have no physical hindrances, and you are a fresh, lively, and beautiful young woman. It only feels intimidating because you've never been with another man before. At least, not that I know of. I wish I knew more about you. I hope you're not some loosey-goosey!"

Uhg! This is so frustrating!

Just breathe, and let your heart guide you. You're not bad at this, and you know more about sex than this body does, so let your instincts guide you.

Heavenly Host, Roderick is so freaking hot!

I'm not cheating! I'm not cheating!

We are soul mates; this is our life, and we might be in different bodies, but admit it! You were always curious. Now's your chance! Go out there and make sweet, passionate love to that gorgeous man! He made so many sacrifices leaving and returning to prove his love. Now go!"

I hustled, gathering my things and grabbing the doorknob before I lost my nerve. I jerked the door open, blasted by a bright light that blinded me.

CHARLIE

I was sitting in the passenger seat of Gregory's red 92' Thunderbird. It was night, and we were making out by the Ohio River levee. While consuming one another in a heated exchange, I broke away from his lips and looked him in the eyes.

"I want you to promise me something," I said.

"What?" Gregory asked.

"A verbal and binding contract with you in which we keep one promise. I'll treat you good as long as you treat me good."

Gregory smiled. "I can agree to that. Did you read the letter I wrote to you?"

I smiled and nodded. "Yes. And I really like you, too," I confessed.

That was not entirely true. My feelings had already evolved into love, but we had only been dating a few weeks, and I didn't want to scare him off with that confession so soon.

Gregory was already making an effort to come to see me every weekend, driving 300 miles roundtrip between Ft. Knox and Ft. Thomas to spend every minute we could get together.

He stayed at his brother's house when I had to work. But he was always there waiting for me the minute I stepped out to the parking lot from my job. Gregory looked sexy as all get out in his Army BDUs. He would open the passenger door of his car, and I'd hop in.

When it got to the point that Gregory was making six-hour roundtrip weekends, we confessed our love for one another. My car trunk would already have a packed weekend bag, and when I parked behind his Thunderbird in front of my mother's house, I'd quickly transfer the bag from my unreliable four-banger to his sleek V6 ride. We'd hug and kiss, then take off to Ft. Knox.

His single-soldier efficiency apartment became our weekend love nest, where we cooked modest meals in the tiny kitchen. We'd spend the rest of our time with our hands all over each other or going places.

We'd celebrated our first birthdays at six months together since they were only a week apart. I thought it would be fun to pose full commando beneath a blanket while holding a birthday cake with numbered candles representing our combined ages. I was twenty, and Gregory was thirty-one, so the candles read fifty-one.

Gregory had set the timer on the camera, ran in all his sexy naked glory back to bed, and slung the blanket over his waist. I pulled the blanket higher and tucked it around me to hide my breasts. We each placed a hand on either side of the platter, lifted the cake proudly before us, and smiled big for the camera.

It was a great picture and a fun memory we would treasure. When we went to pick up our photos at the Kodak shop, the young man behind the counter congratulated us on what he thought was our anniversary. I blushed, and Gregory laughed as the guy gave us a knowing smile and winked.

***

A flash like that from a camera bulb came as a blinding burst, leaving spots before my eyes. I blinked and realized I was back, standing before the door to Roderick's bedroom. I was more nervous than ever as Roderick opened the door wearing only a white sleeveless undershirt and boxer shorts. I took him in, and he eyed me up and down in my white lacey slip.

"So beautiful," he said.

He took the lantern from me and set it on a nearby table. I was shocked when he turned, picked me up, and carried me over the threshold. I squealed as he quickly turned to whisk me inside the room, again closing the door and locking it. An antique Victrola spun a sensual jazzy trumpet melody, and I could still hear the party continue downstairs.

Roderick carried me to the bedside in his strong muscular arms, and I recalled that I was a child the last time anyone lifted my full weight. Gregory was strong, but we matched each other in height and weight, and I always felt self-conscious about allowing him to try. He could pick me up, but not like this!

Roderick set me on my feet, dropped to his knees, and hugged my waist. The action felt so sudden and desperate that I lifted my arms in a surprised reaction as Roderick pressed his nose to the silky garment and deeply breathed me in. I lowered my arms, and my hands relaxed on his head, where I began running my fingers through his thick, soft, dark hair.

I became emotional, remembering what it felt like to be separated from someone you loved for so long. Roderick had been gone for years, whereas Gregory had deployed for months. But the pain was still the same. It was so scary when it came to war because you didn't know if you'd ever seen each other again. Making promises to return was futile because if one's time was up, that was it, which made waiting the most challenging part, not knowing if bad news would arrive at your doorstep.

"Do you think when we make our first child, it'll be a boy or a girl?" Roderick asked.

His question threw me off-guard. "I don't know," I replied. "I do know that he or she will be the best of the both of us."

Roderick nodded. His freshly sprouted facial hair prickled against my flesh beneath my gown. "We will make a beautiful family together."

"We will," I agreed. I already knew this to be true. Not in this lifetime. I didn't know what this life would hold, but I knew the next.

"What do you think they will be like?" he asked. Roderick lifted his head to look at my face. I smiled down at him as I struggled to hold back my tears. He noticed because he stood, sat on the bed, and pulled me to his lap. His thumb stroked my cheeks as the tears broke, and he caught each one.

"What's wrong, Nora?"

A sob let loose from my mouth. This situation wasn't going anything at all like I'd hoped it would. I was missing my future life, the family I knew and loved with all my heart.

Everything was real and certain there, and I felt scared I wouldn't make it back. This moment wouldn't be the hot, sensual do-over love affair with my husband I'd fantasized about. I couldn't let myself give in and let go.

Roderick had to go and initiate the whole starting a family-together conversation. He was just as beautiful inside and out as my Gregory, and he was the closest warm body I had right now.

"I want a beautiful life and children with you, Roderick."

"You look frightened, Nora. Tell me what you're afraid of."

I hiccupped and sniffed, "I know what it's like to have something so beautiful just to take it all for granted and become blindsided, and suddenly it's all ripped away."

"Oh, sweetheart! I'm here now. I promise you; I'm not going anywhere." Roderick placed my hand on his chest above his beating heart as living proof of his vow, and instinctively my palm pressed into the sensation.

"We just don't know that much about each other. I feel like I don't even know myself at all," I confessed.

"Then tell me what you do know, Nora: the good, the bad, the beautiful, the ugly. I want to know you. All of you."

Good Lord! I wanted to kiss this man.

But I needed to get everything off my chest first. I would be no good to Roderick this way, and he was a man who deserved to be loved fully. I mean, at least from what I have gathered so far, he seemed like an honorable and loyal man. This was what my heart told me. He was willing to fight for freedom and love, which required great strength and courage. I felt I possessed neither of those qualities. My soul finally got to wear the lovely shell I desired, but it was useless if what mattered in my mind didn't match up. It made my intentions feel like a charade.

"Do you believe in soul mates?" I asked.

"Of course I do. We are soul mates. Don't you feel it, Nora?" Roderick tucked my hair behind my ear and stroked my cheek.

"I do," I admitted. Goosebumps prickled my flesh, and I shivered.

"Are you cold?" he asked.

I shook my head. "Not physically." Shamefully, I bit my lips after the words slipped out.

Roderick's brows pinched together, and he looked mildly irritated. "How could you say that about yourself?"

I couldn't answer that. I looked up at the ceiling and sighed. "I apologize a lot," I admitted.

“Sorry?” Roderick quipped. I met his eyes, filled with mischief.

“You remind me of someone,” I said.

“Who?” he asked.

“Do you believe in reincarnation, as in people living again in another life?” I asked.

“I’m not so sure about that one. I’d like to think we move on, go home. You know?” Roderick pointed up.

“I do too. I still do. But up until recently, I think I may have stumbled into the possibility that it is more than probable. I feel like I’m living it right now.”

“So, are you saying I remind you of someone from a past life?”

“No, not a past life,” I admitted. Roderick looked confused, so I elaborated.

“Let’s say *theoretically*, our souls are capable of moving forward or backward through time. Instead of remembering a past life, that soul still holds onto the memories of its next life. Somewhere in the future.”

“You have me intrigued, Mrs. Akner. I am your willing student. Continue.” Roderick grinned. He bounced me on his knees, and I had to hold onto his broad shoulders to keep my butt from sliding off his lap and smacking the floor.

“At ease, Sargent Akner,” I snapped in command.

Roderick growled in approval. “Yes, ma’am!” His knees stopped, and he wrapped his strong arms around my waist to pull me closer. He whispered in my ear, “*Continue*,” and I felt gooseflesh erupt on my arms and legs. Despite my reservations, I melted into him like putty in his capable hands.

"So, say I already know or have lived our next life together. It sounds unbelievable. But I could tell you how we met when we married, how many children we have, and all the details I know about our family."

"You're going to try to convince me this isn't some story, that it has already happened in the future? How would you go about proving something like that?" he asked.

"Well, I know people will produce and televise multiple documentaries about World War II. Televisions will be in more than half of American homes by the mid-1950s, and people will watch those documentaries in their homes instead of at the theaters. Oh, and movies! Hundreds of films will be made."

What else? I thought to myself.

"The presidents! Uhm, Roosevelt. Truman was president until 1953. After him, Eisenhower, Kennedy, Johnson, Nixon, Ford, Carter, Reagan."

"Whoa, whoa, whoa! Nora! Most of those names don't mean anything to me. How do you know all of this?" Roderick whispered the question.

"Because the person you remind me of is a history buff and especially fascinated with World War II. And I had to memorize the presidents in my first year of high school. It's all I can remember, along with the details of my future life. I honestly know nothing about you or myself in this life. My memory only goes back to when you spoke to me in the hallway less than an hour ago."

"You're joking," he said.

I shook my head. "I'm seriously not."

"Who is this person who reminds you of me?"

I struggled to say it because I knew he would take it wrong. But he had to know.

"He's. My husband."

Roderick's eyes bugged out. "Your husband? Nora, what are you saying? Did you meet someone else while I was gone? All your letters! You said you still wanted to be my wife, that you'd wait for me, no matter how long. Have you changed your mind?"

My eyes bugged out. "What? No! Roderick! You and he are one in the same soul—my soul mate. You said you believed! We will be together now, and we will be together again in our next lives. I love you; I can feel it in my soul, but I'm telling you the truth when I say I can't remember our lives before tonight. I don't know how Nora feels, but I'm guessing she does love you very much."

"Sweetheart, did you hit your head? Are you suffering from amnesia? I have seen that happen to a few soldiers first-hand. It usually clears up and a few weeks or months. Do we need to see a doctor?"

I huffed in frustration. "No, Roderick! I assure you I'm fine. Well, other than my head feeling a little achy. But my body in the future is still clinging to life. I thought I'd died. Gregory, and our youngest, Sarah, are still waiting for me to wake up, and I don't know how I'm supposed to get back to them!"

"Do you want to leave me?" Roderick asked.

"Uhg! Good grief, husband! You are just as oblivious now as you are in the future. I have to explain everything to you in minute detail and multiple times before you understand what's going on inside my head!"

"Nora, none of this makes any sense!" Roderick exasperated.

"And you think it makes sense to me? I wish I had a better explanation. I really do! All I can think is this is some kind of test. I wasn't exactly taking good care of myself. I've struggled with depression for most of my life. But, you! You have always stayed by my side, and I have yours. So, no, Roderick. I would never leave you! I don't want anyone but you."

"And this Gregory?"

"Is you! Dammit, Roddy!"

Roderick laughed.

"What?" I asked snippily.

"That is what you called me. In your letters."

"Roddy?" I smiled. "I didn't know that."

"You did. I can show you." He lifted me off his lap with so much ease it startled me. I also found it arousing. He deposited my rear end on the bed and stood. I admired his muscular back, glutes, arms, and legs as he crossed the room to retrieve something from his duffel bag. He returned with two large stacks of letters bound together with twine and set them on the bed beside me.

My eyes widened. "Wow! I did write! A lot!"

Roderick chuckled. "You really don't remember?"

Remorsefully, I shook my head. "I'm so sorry."

"Nora, you said your head hurts. Are you sure you didn't have a fall or something and woke up with amnesia?"

I shrugged my shoulders. "How would I know if I did? I mean, it could be something my future body is experiencing, and it's the cause of all of this."

"That's plausible, I suppose." Roderick rubbed the stubble on his chin as he considered the possibility.

"So, you believe me?" I asked.

"You've never led me to believe you'd be untruthful or unfaithful, for that matter," he replied.

"But you said we barely knew one another."

"I know that. But when we met, I swear, it felt like I knew you my entire life." Roderick extended the letters to me.

I smiled. "May I?"

"You wrote them, whether you remember or not. Be my guest."

I accepted the letters from Roderick, and he went to prop a couple of pillows against the metal bedframe. He sat to my right and gestured for me to join him. I chuckled.

"What?" He smiled.

"You sleep on the right side in our next life too."

"Really?" He grinned.

I nodded enthusiastically. I scooched my butt back to join my husband and settled the stacks of letters between my legs. As I leaned against the pillow, my slip rose above my knees, and Roderick growled approvingly. Heat rose inside my belly, and I laughed. "You growl the same."

Roderick grinned. "Are your legs as gorgeous as they are now in our next life?"

My head dropped in shame. I shook it like I wanted not to envision what my body looked like. The anxiety crept in, and I said, "I don't want to talk about it."

Roderick's hand went to my knee. "Nora."

I sniffed. "Yeah?"

"How long have we been married?"

"In this life?" I asked.

"No. You know what I'm asking," Roderick replied briskly.

"Twenty-eight years," I said.

"That's wonderful! Nora, you must be doing something to keep me interested."

"Not really," I admitted. "I feel like you stay with me out of a sense of duty. For better or worse, you are a stickler for rules, especially safety protocol. You're kind of anal about certain things."

Roderick burst into laughter. "Nora! Did your mother or father let you speak like that? My goodness, woman!"

"Sorry, I kinda forgot what era it was. Believe me when I tell you our daughter, Sarah is so much worse." I looked at Roderick, and his eyes softened.

"We have a daughter named Sarah?"

I nodded. "And a son named Ben. And Sarah is a twin to our daughter Olivia. They're not identical. In fact, Olivia looks more like Ben."

"Wow! I hope we'll be parents in this life too. I want to experience that with you."

I placed my hand on Roderick's. "I want that too."

"I like the names we chose. Do you think we could use those names?"

"I don't see why not. The girls are named after their grandmothers; our son has your father's name."

"How old are they now?"

"The girls are sixteen, and our boy is nineteen."

"And you put up with me for twenty-eight years?" Roderick's jaw dropped in fascination, and I laughed.

"That's one of our many running jokes," I admitted.

"I believe that." Roderick smiled.

"Oh, believe me, I haven't been easy."

I had committed a few blunders while trying to find some niche' in which I could contribute to the household. I fell victim to a couple of scammers and felt guilty and stupid for causing such a mess. I constantly struggled with my identity, trying to figure out who I was beyond the titles of a wife and a mother. It wasn't till after my mother passed that I started writing. But the fear of success superseded my willingness to put myself out there. Self-sabotage was a side effect of depression and anxiety.

"Don't fault yourself, darling. We all make mistakes. Nobody's perfect."

"I know. But over the last several years, I've let myself go. This young, beautiful face and body are not what you're going to get in our next life together."

"Nora! You've been married to me. Me! For twenty-eight years! You've taken care of me and three children. So, make that four children. I'm so sorry, sweetheart. I probably haven't been there for you like I should have. And I'm certain you are absolutely beautiful. Besides, I bet I'm pretty rough around the edges. How old are we?"

"You're fifty-eight, and I'm forty-seven."

"We have an eleven-year age gap? I suppose that's not so bad."

"It isn't," I agreed. "But I was twenty, and you were thirty-one when we got married, and some of your fellow soldier friends used to ask if I was your daughter."

Roderick laughed. "Well, I suppose that says something about my looks."

"Stop it!" I shoved playfully at his shoulder. "Nobody asks that question anymore. They haven't for a long time."

"So, you caught up with me?"

"In the old age department? Definitely! But you still act like a toddler sometimes."

"What is your name?"

"Rachael," I replied. "My maiden name is Tanner. We are Mr. and Mrs. Gregory Samuel Talbert."

"When were we born? What year is it now?" Roderick drew my fingers between his. I sucked in a breath and tried to distract myself from the growing feeling of need firing inside my belly.

"Are you sure you want to know? Knowing when our timeline will end in this life would damper the mood." I felt an ache in my chest from that thought. Roderick would die between now and the mid-60s, and me, Nora, before the mid-70s.

"So? We will live this life to the fullest," Roderick declared.

"Yeah, but we're not doing a fantastic job of it in our next life," I admitted.

"It can't be all that bad." Roderick released my hand and began stroking my leg.

I sucked in another shaky breath. "Don't."

"Don't what?" He smiled.

"Be so…you right now!"

"What do you mean?" he asked innocently. But by the look in his eyes, I knew.

I gave him a challenging glare. "You are an insatiable horn dog!"

Roderick laughed. "A horn dog? Me?"

"Yes, you!"

"Then we must be doing something right. How did our wedding night go?"

"I feel like you already know the answer to that question, Mr. Akner."

Roderick's smile was handsomely impish.

"Did we consummate our marriage before you left for the war?" I asked.

"We didn't have time. It all happened so fast. We met in Newport, dated for three weeks, and fell madly in love. I got the orders to leave, and we went to the Justice of Peace in Elizabethtown the next day. I was on the bus leaving an hour later."

"Elizabethtown!" I nearly jumped out of my skin.

"Yes. Your mother was there. She was overjoyed."

"What about my father?"

"Nora, your father passed away when you were young."

I was dumbfounded—all the similarities were mind-blowing. It was like God was pinpointing the right direction on the map, but our free will kept leading us off course. And here we were, cycling through rinse and repeat.

"Roderick," I sat up further. "Gregory and I got married in the Elizabethtown courthouse by the Justice of Peace. My mother wasn't there, but she knew you would marry me. I was very sick once when we were dating. You drove twenty miles over the speed limit to get to me and got pulled over by the police. Mom knew it was love that drove you to get to me. She thought so highly of you and wished God had made copies of you for my sisters. But my dad, he passed when I was ten. This is so very,"

"Meant to be," Roderick finished. "Rachael, I believe you. I'm so sorry for my doubt."

"It's okay. I understand. I'm still having a hard time with it myself. Wait a minute! OMG! Did you call me Rachael?"

Roderick looked at me quizzically, "Yes, I did. And what does OMG mean?"

"It's an acronym for Oh My God, or Oh My Goodness."

"Yes, that abbreviation works for this situation," he agreed. "Rachael?" he repeated my name.

"Hm?" I was looking down at the letters but then looked back at him.

Roderick squeezed my hand, "I want to know you in this life and the next."

I looked into Roderick's eyes, and my lips quivered. "Me too."

How did I get so blessed? Twice? The floodgates broke, and I cried tears of joy. And still, deep down, I believed I didn't deserve him.

"I don't deserve you, Rachael. You're soul. I can see it now in your eyes. Why did it take me so long?"

I chuckled, having heard him say the same thing I was thinking. I shook my head and said, "I don't know. We're both old fools! It went both ways when I told you I had to explain things repeatedly. I've been pretty guilty of my mind drifting and not hearing you lately."

"Probably because I'm old and talk about the same things over and over again."

I laughed. "You do that quite a bit."

Roderick smiled. "Do you think we'll ever get it right?"

"I don't know. But I'm willing to keep trying as long as you are."

"I'm up for the challenge. Rachael, I'll never give up on you. Promise me the same."

"It's hard to keep promises, Roderick. I've always been faithful to you. I've been struggling with depression since my mom passed away, but I love you, and I will try my best."

My husband leaned forward to kiss me. He gave me a stern look and said, "Then you need to tell me to get me ass in gear and do more to help you."

I laughed and put my hands on his face to pull him closer. "You've always been there for me." I kissed him with meaning, letting him know my words were true. Heat spread through my core, and something occurred to me that I had to ask. I broke the kiss and said, "Wait! If we never consummated our marriage, am I a virgin? Did I tell you whether or not I've been with anyone else?"

"I met your mother, and she took a liking to me right away. She's a sweet woman with a no-nonsense personality. She said you were a lady and warned me I'd better put a ring on your finger before I left. It was important to maintain your virtue by doing the right thing first. Sweetheart, I'm sorry I didn't save myself for you, but that was long before we met, and I promise to be kind to your body for our first time together."

I smiled, observing the simple gold wedding band on my finger, turning it back and forth between my finger and thumb.

"You were my first time in our future life," I said. "And since then, we've had some fun. Especially in our younger BC years."

"What's BC?" Roderick asked.

"Before Children," I smiled.

"You are a funny woman. No wonder we've been together for so long."

"You're funny, too," I pointed out. "I always found your sense of humor attractive. I did ask God for a man who could make me laugh."

"I have a great personality. Wonderful! Just how lacking am I in looks?" Roderick asked jestfully.

I laughed and responded, "One of your all-time favorite sayings was, 'I don't have looks or money, so it must be love.' You didn't seem to believe me when I told you how handsome you are."

"Much like you don't believe me when I tell you how beautiful you are. Nora, I mean Rachael, we sound like we both could use a wake-up call. I don't understand why you don't see yourself as God, or I see you. You are wonderful and fearfully made, both inside and out."

"I've been too slow to catch on for some time now. I need to start taking better care of myself. If I ever wake up. Our children need both of us. We make a good team."

"We are a *great* team," Roderick agreed. He reached between my legs to move the letters.

"Hey!" I protested, "I still want to read those!"

"You will. But first, may I hold you for a while, Mrs. Akner, and see if it takes us anywhere? If you still want to wait, I promise you, I'm not going anywhere."

"That is a promise no one can guarantee, Mr. Akner. As you can see by *my* being *here*, tomorrow is not guaranteed."

"I understand, Rachael. You can call me Gregory if you wish. It makes no difference to me as long as it's your voice."

DELTA

Roderick held me in his arms, and we spent most of our first night talking and getting to know each other. I told him more about our future life, and he shared what he knew about this one. I read a few of the letters Nora sent him. Her undying devotion to Roderick and the heartache she felt missing him were as comparable and passionate to my feelings for Gregory. We spent some time kissing, and holding back was becoming increasingly difficult as our desire rose in tangible increments.

The soft caresses and tender kisses he placed on my body felt pleasingly familiar yet different. We were on an exhilarating voyage, and Nora's young body, untainted by the ravages of time, responded magically to his every touch. He held back as he waited for me to initiate going any further. And though I found myself falling in love with him all over again, there was still this reservation inside of me, wondering if Nora's conscious would remember their first night together after I was gone.

I had this cautionary feeling in my soul that I would not reside in my current state of awareness for the entirety of Roderick's and Nora's lives together.

My soul clung to my future vessel like a weighted anchor of hope. And sometimes, when I closed my eyes, I visualized my still lying form in the hospital bed. The beeping monitor echoed in the abyss of my mind, and I could feel rough hands stroking and clinging to mine like a phantom's touch.

"Racheal," Gregory's voice called from beyond this time and place. *"Please come back to me. I need you."*

"I'm coming," I called back.

When I opened my eyes, Roderick was looking down at me.

"We call to each other through the passages of time."

I blinked and nodded. Tears trailed down my cheeks. "He needs me," I replied with a hoarse breath.

"I need you," Roderick said adamantly.

My fingers brushed his cheek. "Nora will still be here. Though I may not remember this night tomorrow, I hope she will."

"It is tomorrow," Roderick pointed to the window where sunlight streaked between the small gap of the drawn curtains, "And you're still here."

It was so quiet now.

"The party downstairs and everyone celebrating outside?" I asked. "It's 1945, right?"

"It is. What did your historical documentaries tell you about this time?"

"I remember the newspaper image of a kiss shared in Time Square between a Navy sailor and a nurse. That picture became iconic throughout the decades."

Roderick sat up and began to get dressed.

"Where are you going?" I asked.

“Get dressed. I’m taking my wife out to breakfast.”

My stomach rumbled, and I couldn’t disagree with my husband’s suggestion. I turned away from him to push the top half of my slip down so I could put my bra back on. I was still feeling modest since we hadn’t yet consummated our marriage. We needed to remedy it, but I thought it would be selfish of me to steal Nora’s moment. A treasured memory she could recall.

I pulled on my dress and turned to see Roderick appraising me with a smirk on his handsome face. I felt my cheeks flare, and he laughed. “Still feeling shy after last night, Mrs. Akner? He pulled me into his arms and kissed my lips.

I looked to the side shyly. “We still haven’t done the deed,” I replied.

Roderick nudged my chin with his finger, and I lifted my eyes to his. “We’ll have to take care of that later.” He smiled. “But first, our bodies require fuel. Come, wife!” He slapped his flat stomach. “Your husband requires sustenance!”

I laughed. “You can still make this girl laugh.”

“And the sound of your laughter drives me to continue to do so. I’m going downstairs to check on the bar. Meet me down there when you’re ready, Mrs. Akner.” At that, Roderick went through the door, and I heard his footsteps trotting down the stairs with all the clattering of a joyous Clydesdale.

I went to the bathroom to freshen up. Using the toilet, I wondered where I could obtain certain items. I found most of what I needed in the mirrored vanity cabinet on the wall. I brushed my teeth with the toothbrush and Pepsodent toothpaste. I could use a tutorial right then as I struggled to figure out how to do my hair and makeup the way it had been last night. I ran a comb through my hair, pinned it to the best of my ability, and applied the Bésame black cream mascara and rose-colored lipstick I found. A light dusting of powder foundation later, and I was heading down the staircase in anticipation of seeing the outside world of this bygone era.

I found Roderick in the midst of disgruntled muttering about the state of the bar as he bussed one of the tables. It looked like people had a pretty great time last night. I cleared my throat, his head whipped around to look at me, and he smiled.

"Looks like a great party," I stated.

"I'm glad we stayed upstairs last night. Most soldiers can hold their liquor but not their mouths. Seeing a beautiful dame like yourself, they'd turn into a bunch of fools. If they got too close to my bride, I'd have to punch a few ugly mugs in their sour mouths."

"So, we live above a bar?" I asked.

"Our bar, my dear," Roderick replied.

"Our bar?" I asked in surprise.

"It's been passed down through the family, and ever since we both signed our marriage contract, it became yours as well. Look." Roderick took my hand and led me to a framed paper on the wall. He pointed it out and beamed with pride.

"Well, I'll be!" I read the marriage certificate on the wall.

"This is to certify that on the 9th day of October 1942, the rites of matrimony were legally solemnized between Roderick Gregory Akner and Nora Lynn Nasaw at the Elizabeth County Courthouse in Hardin County in the presence of George A. Tanner and Judith C. Mayhurst."

"Judith is your mother," Roderick pointed. "She remarried a few years after your father passed. Her husband was working the oil rigs off the Alabama coast and couldn't make it."

Absentmindedly, I nodded. That information didn't strike a chord with me. Although seeing the same day Gregory and I married blew my mind. And what shocked me more than that was seeing my father's handwritten name signed as a witness on my marriage certificate, I pointed, and Roderick looked closer.

"George is my best friend. We didn't serve together in Italy. He served on a ship in the merchant marines. I haven't seen him since we left, but I hope he'll be home soon."

"Roderick!" I said again as I tightly clutched his sleeve in my fist and shook his arm. Tremulous emotions welled inside me, threatening to erupt. My lips quaked, and tears sprung from my eyes. My sweet husband handed me his handkerchief, and I dabbed at the frantic tears.

"What's wrong, Nora? I would call you Rachael, but people know you as Nora, so I don't want to confuse anybody."

I waved away his concern. "Never mind that. ***That!***" I pointed again. "Is my father's name."

"Your father? George is a few years younger than you. What do you mean?" Roderick's eyes widened with realization. "Ohhh! George Tanner is *YOUR* father!"

I nodded. "Roderick. You can't tell him. I mean, if we see him. I might lose my shit. But he can't know who *I* am."

"He'd called me crazy anyway. And you and George have already met. He witnessed our wedding, as you can see."

"My father saw me get married! Do you have any idea how incredible that is? He died when I was ten years old! He didn't get to see us get married in the future."

"Wow!" Roderick stared, amazed for a long moment. Then he turned to me and asked, "Lose your shit?"

I burst into laughter. "It's slang for losing your mind, being overcome with panic."

"I've seen the apes sling their shit at the Cincinnati Zoo. Then they would jump up and down, hooting and hollering like they lost it and wanted it back." Roderick said it so matter-of-factly with a straight face that it finally sunk in after a silent pause.

When his lips pulled back into a smug grin, I burst again, laughing like a hyena-donkey hybrid and snorting like a pig. I clutched my stomach, and he had to hold me upright so I wouldn't collapse to the floor and die in my fit of laughter.

I laughed so long and hard; I thought I might pee my panties or pass out. Good thing Nora's bladder had excellent control. My inability to calm myself made Roderick join in, and the situation turned preposterous as the bell above the door rang when someone opened it behind us.

PAPA

"Hello?" a young male voice called.

I didn't see who it was right away. But Roderick's laughter died quickly, and he gently shook me. "Nora!"

"Wha-What?" I held my breath, trying to stifle my insanity.

"He's here!" Roderick whispered.

"Who's here?" I chuckled. I looked up and froze.

Roderick stepped in front of me. He took hold of my shoulders, getting my attention; he said, "There's a ladies' room down that hallway to the right. He firmly pressed the handkerchief into my hand. "You might need a moment." He nodded in the direction of the hallway.

I glanced at the man watching us from across the room. I had seen pictures of my father when he was younger. They were in black and white. Yet here he stood in 4D and full breath-taking color. He looked so handsome, and I couldn't help the breath I sucked in. I began to shake. I wanted to jump across the tables like a crazed gazelle, throw my arms around him, and cry.

I shifted in his direction, and Roderick held me back. "Nora. I wish you could go to him that way, but you can't. George might not know what to make of you rushing to him and crying in his arms. He might punch my lights out thinking I hurt or insulted you."

Nodding, I turned away before my facial expression contorted with frightfully morose joy and went around the corner to the hallway. Roderick stepped forward to greet my father with a brotherly hug.

"Welcome home, Georgie!"

"Welcome home, Roddy! Sorry, I missed the party last night. We just got off the bus this morning. Is Nora okay? I thought she'd be happy to see me."

"She is. She's just feeling overwhelmed with happiness at my being home. Give her a moment."

I peeked around the corner to spy on them and jerked back as my father looked in my direction.

"Poor gal. I can imagine. There were a lot of guys blubbering like sad saps over their women on the ship. I wish I was that sorely missed."

Oh, Dad. If you only knew! I thought.

I peeked around the corner, watching their warm exchange, which filled my heart with joy. Even in death, I knew my father liked Gregory. And to see that he and Roderick were best friends in this life made me understand why. They acted more like brothers as their conversation bordered slapstick humiliation throwing insults at one another.

Shortly after Gregory and I married, my father had come to me in a dream that felt so real; I could smell the popcorn and cotton candy in the air long after I woke.

We were walking down my childhood street, surrounded by a vision of pink. Not a single shade of pink, but multiple shades of the color so vivid one could only imagine a variety so inconceivable within the realm of the conscious world. Ahead of us was a carnival with all the rides and games. Balloons floated around us and seemed to follow us as if listening to our conversation.

"I miss you, Daddy. You've been gone so long."

"I know, baby girl. But I'm here now to tell you something." He plucked a bubble gum pink balloon from the air and held the string out to me. I smiled and accepted. Holding onto the balloon suddenly made my heart feel lighter.

"I wanted to tell you how proud I am of you and the choices you've made in your life." My father's admission sparked joy.

I smiled brightly, never wanting our walk to end. It felt like a divine winged stallion might come galloping up at any moment, and we'd ride across a rainbow-filled sky together.

"Thank you, Daddy. I miss you so much. I've always wanted to make you proud."

"Always. I also wanted to tell you how much I like and approve of your husband. He's a good man who treats my little girl as she deserves. Hang on to him, sweetheart. Good men are hard to find. And in this world, you need love to survive."

My heart felt so warm; I thought I'd sail into the air. We continued walking until everything began to fade, and I woke up. That dream felt like a lifeline in the darkness.

A few days later, I told my mom about it, and she told me something I never knew about my father.

"I never mentioned this to you before because I hadn't thought about it in such a long time," she said.

"What is it?" I asked.

"Your father was a carny. He'd work with the traveling carnivals setting them up and breaking them down."

My mother's admission struck me with awe, and that's when I knew my dream was more than a dream. My father came to visit me. I told Gregory about it, and he didn't call me out as a superstitious loon. He was happy to hear that my dad approved of him.

I continued to spy on Roderick, and my father engaged in a happy bantering, not wanting to pull away for fear I'd never see either of them again. My stomach growled loudly, and George asked, "Are you keeping a circus bear behind the bar?"

Roderick laughed. "No. Nora and I were getting ready to go out for breakfast. Want to come along?"

Yes! Please! My heart zinged with anticipation at getting to spend time with both of the men I loved. I needed to quit thinking of George as my dad. He wasn't in this life, which made me sad, but at the same time, I'd take him as a part of my life any way I could, and his friendship was the next best thing.

I didn't want to slip up or break down in front of him, either. I couldn't. One of his many sayings was, 'Don't cry over me after I'm gone.' This opportunity to know him twice in his lifetime was a gift I didn't want to squander by behaving like a fool and crying incessantly. My dad was a brave man, but he never liked seeing a female in distress.

One night I was crying in my sleep, and my mother came and swaddled my little four-year-old body in my black and yellow tartan blanket. My father had just arrived home from his third shift job as a machinist. My mom carried me to the dining room and deposited me in my father's waiting arms. He cradled and sang to me, calling me his 'little blonde bombshell.' In that moment, I felt so safe and treasured. I'd settled peacefully back into calm slumber to his soothing voice.

"You're going to be a wonderful father one day," I whispered from my hiding place around the corner.

I desperately wanted to warn him of the dangers he'd face in the future, like his near-fatal motorcycle accident, which had kept him in the hospital for weeks after my mother had given birth to my baby sister in the same hospital one floor below.

But somehow, in my mind, I knew it might inextricably alter the lines of fate. Did I wish my father had lived well into my adult years?

Yes.

Of course, I did. And even though I was being gifted this opportunity by who knows what supernatural force, I knew I must bite my tongue on the matter.

Would he even heed or remember my warning thirty-five years from now anyway? I doubted it. It's not like I knew how much longer I'd be here myself in Nora's body.

Roderick looked back in my direction, and I slid behind the wall. It was then I decided to use the bathroom and pull myself together. After splashing water on my face and cleaning away the smudges under my eyes from tears of sorrow and laughter, I returned to the bar where George's kind brown eyes met mine.

"There she is!" He greeted me congenially. "The gorgeous woman who managed to lock a ball and chain around my buddy's neck. Since you two got hitched, he hasn't been able to walk upright."

I laughed at his jibe. Dad always had a great sense of humor. I remembered how funny he was from my youth. He rose to his six-foot height and opened his arms for a hug, and I stopped, unsure if I'd start crying again once I put my arms around him and, even more uncertain, if I'd be able to let him go.

Roderick stepped in and turned it into a group hug. Which granted me some restraint as he kneaded my shoulder, letting me know he was there for me.

"We're all family now. Right, Nora?" George asked.

He might lose his load if he only knew how close to the truth that statement was. It would be a few years before he met his first wife and had my half-sisters and brothers. He and my mother wouldn't meet till the late sixties when a strange twist of fate would match the two together. But that was a whole other highly complex story many people wouldn't understand, given their extreme age gap and dire existential circumstances.

"We are family," I agreed. "Welcome home," I swallowed back a sob, "George."

George noticed the apprehensiveness in my voice, and he gently patted my back. "Awe, Nora. Did you miss me? I gotta say, if Roddy here hadn't spotted you first, you'd be my little blonde bombshell."

Oh crap! He had to go and say it! It was an innocent jest on his part, as technically, I wasn't his daughter. Still, I turned and ran to the ladies' room, burst through the door, clutched the sink with my hands shaking uncontrollably, and burst into tears.

I heard my father's concerned muffled voice. "What did I do? Was it something I said?"

"I don't know," Roderick replied. "She was talking about her father before you arrived. He passed away, and I think he may have *called* her his little blond bombshell or something along those lines."

Bingo, I thought. Roderick was well attuned to my emotional triggers. He caught on quickly, and I loved him all the more for it.

"She lost her father?" George asked. "I'm sorry, I didn't know. Is it all right if I talk to her and give her a hug? I don't like seeing a woman cry. I'm a sensitive guy."

"If she wants," Roderick said. And hearing his consent through the door was all I needed, as I immediately opened it and flew to my father.

"Nora, I'm so sorry for your lo," George hadn't finished getting the words out before I threw my arms around his waist and balled. His arms came around me in a tight warm hug, and every emotion came full circle. I remembered the moment my mother woke me and said, "Daddy has gone to be with Jesus."

I was ten years old, and I knew what that meant. My daddy was gone from the world, taken too soon. At fifty-eight years old, the same age my Gregory, he'd suffered a cerebral vascular hemorrhage as he walked up to accept an award at work. Just before he shook his boss's hand, he collapsed. He was in a coma overnight at the hospital and died at nine a.m. the following day.

My mom, sisters, and I struggled with his loss. The whole neighborhood missed him. We were poor, but my father was a generous man. He loved kids, and we'd walk new friends into the house without needing to ask. He'd asked their names and told them to hold out one hand and keep their fingers up on the other. He'd place a handful of butterscotch candies in one hand and stack pretzel loops on their fingers. It always brought smiles to our friends' faces. And no matter the skin color of those faces, my dad welcomed and treated them all the same.

My father was no saint. He had his flaws, but he was my dad. The best dad we girls could ever hope for.

"Can I tell you something?" He asked as he rocked me side to side, still holding on to me. I wasn't letting go either, but I nodded into his shoulder.

"God sends his angels to help mend our broken hearts. He gives us tears to cleanse our sorrows. And he always provides us with what we need when we need it the most. You may have lost your father, but God sent you a good man to love and be loved. Family is our greatest treasure here on Earth, and as long as we have family to remember us, we will live on forever."

I remembered him saying those words to my mother, sisters, and me when I was young. And here he was, so young and refined with wisdom that I knew the Holy Ghost filled him at this moment to give me the words I needed, straight from the mouth of my visiting guardian angel brought back to flesh.

And in this healing moment, I realized I could finally let him go. Granted, he would always be in my heart, just as I would in my husband and children.

It made me wonder if it was actually my time to go in the future and if I was living my life in review from my past to the present before I could let go and continue my journey. But there was still something in me that doubted because I felt there was something I needed to do first.

"You should have been an Army Chaplain," Roderick said. I felt my husband's hand rubbing circles on my back, and with some lingering reluctance, I let my father go.

"I'm no saint," George said to Roderick. "Are you going to be okay?" he asked me.

I looked into his beautiful chestnut eyes and nodded. "I am now. Thank you. Your hug and words meant more to me than you'll ever know."

"Good! I'm glad I could help." He pulled a handkerchief from his back pocket and handed it to me. I wiped the tears away and blew my nose in it, and George winced. "You can keep that."

"Sorry," I laughed. Little did he know, I had no intention of giving it back to him otherwise. If I could carry it back to the future and hold onto it forever, I would, snot, tears, and all. It smelled like him, that familiar smell that took me back to my childhood when I sat on his knee, and we'd have silly conversations and sing songs together into the microphone. He kept an audio journal on cassette tapes to document our lives as people would do with video cameras. My dad was a pioneer before the conception of podcasting was such a thing, telling stories, covering current events, and conducting interviews.

Years later, looking at a picture where he wore a suit jacket and tie, hearing his words made me realize how wise he was beyond his years. He was a simple man who had lived a simple life, and his sentimentality was refreshing and humbling. His stories were his adventures, and he told them in bucketloads.

UNIFORM

I may have spilled enough tears to fill two rivers converging into a delta. The echoes of the past had come back to me in shockwaves of epic proportions, causing my soul to pour heavily. I felt emotionally wrung as I exited the ladies' room, having cleaned my face again. I'd forgone reapplying any makeup, remembering how my dad always said a woman shouldn't cover her natural beauty.

"Ready for breakfast?" Roderick asked.

"I'm starving," I said despite the knot in my stomach.

We made our way to a diner down the street, and I recognized the street names and the familiar architecture. We were in Covington, Kentucky, next to Newport, where Roderick and I had met. It wasn't a far walk, but it was a muggy summer morning, and air conditioning consisted of fans and open windows. Before we entered the diner, a young man yelled from the sidewalk. "Newspaper! Get your newspaper here!"

"I'll take one." Roderick gave the guy a coin and received his paper. George held the door for me, and I smiled. I had to restrain my urge to hug him again, and it still ached to push down my love for my dad in the cockles of my heart. I focused on the smells of freshly brewed coffee, bacon, and eggs.

We sat at a booth with Roderick directly across from George. Maintaining his relaxed demeanor despite everything he knew about George and me being father and daughter, Roderick unfolded the newspaper, and my eyes widened as I saw the freshly printed iconic image I had mentioned earlier.

A waitress came to take our order, and George immediately started flirting with her. She blushed and giggled as she wrote his order on her notepad, and when she got to me, she asked, "What'll you have, sweetheart?"

"The regular breakfast platter and some coffee, please."

I don't know why I asked for coffee. I wasn't a coffee drinker, but I'd said it like it was a consistency in my daily life. Roderick stirred a few spoons of sugar into his and nearly spilled the piping-hot liquid on his lap as he brought it to his lips. His focus on the newspaper's front page had him looking like he'd seen a ghost. Which was his reply when George asked, "What's the matter?"

"I think I just saw a ghost," Roderick said hauntedly.

I can relate to that statement, I thought to myself.

"In the newspaper?" George asked.

"Yes." Roderick pointed to a random guy in the background of the iconic picture, though I felt confident he'd probably never seen the man in his entire life. He looked at me, and I confirmed with a nod. His eyes widen in disbelief. But as I've said before, seeing is believing, and with each passing revelation, we both believed more and more.

"What makes you say he's a ghost?" Dad, I mean, George asked.

"Because I saw a guy who looked just like him in passing, and a few days later, he was carried away on a stretcher." Roderick made a slitting sound while dragging his thumb across his throat, indicating the man's demise. It seemed he was as good at spinning tales as my father.

"Well, that's frightening. And I've seen my share of fright," George admitted.

"We all have," Roderick agreed. "I'm so glad we're home. And I'm even happier to be here with the two best people I know."

"I'll drink to that," George raised his coffee cup.

Roderick and I followed.

"To a roof over our heads, the clothes on our backs. The air in our lungs and the enemy sacked. Here's to victory!" George toasted.

"To victory," Roderick and I echoed. We clinked our mugs and took a sip.

We sat in the diner for over an hour, and I was fascinated hearing my dad's stories. He was always a good storyteller, and I attributed my acquired skills to his teaching. It was a refreshing experience hearing about life and what was happening in the world from the horse's mouth instead of reading it on an electronic device. People were more engaged with one another. Humanity felt more connected.

We left the diner and walked for a while. George stopped at an alleyway. He pulled a camera out of the holder he was carrying around his neck and said, "Let's get some pictures."

"Okay," Roderick agreed.

"You and Nora get together first," George instructed. I didn't think anything of it as I sidled up to Roderick, and he put his arm around me.

"Say cheese," George encouraged.

"CHEESE!" I felt a big smile stretch across my face. This day couldn't be any better. I was here with the two best people I knew and loved. I didn't know anyone else in this life. I couldn't even say I knew who my mother was. According to Roderick, the woman named Judith, who'd given birth to Nora, didn't live close by, and I didn't know if I'd get the chance to meet her. I imagined she was kind and beautiful, but the idea of her felt foreign to me. I didn't know if her soul would be the same as my mom in the future.

One thing was certain. My mom was the best mom in any lifetime a woman could get. Aside from my husband, she was my hero in so many respects.

After my dad passed away, my mom went to school and worked full-time while raising five girls, keeping a roof over our heads and our bellies fed.

They say it takes a village, and our neighborhood was just that. Our closest neighbors pitched in to help ensure we were safe at home while she had to work her butt off so we could make it.

When Dad had his motorcycle accident, she went to visit him. Having just given birth to baby girl number five, she told him she needed him to stay. Despite all the doctors saying he wouldn't make it through the night, he'd heard her in his near-death unconscious state and woke a few days later.

It was a grueling five years he remained on this Earth; each day, his body experienced so much pain that he prayed God would take him home. Yet, he still worked to provide for his family till that fateful day when his body could take no more.

By then, my mother's resilience had grown, having to take care of five girls and be his helper more than he could hers, and when Dad lay in a coma, she gave her blessing for him to go home. And despite the doctors saying there was a chance he'd wake?

Let's just say doctors don't know everything.

My youngest sister was five years old by then and able to attend school, which made it feasible for our mother to do the same. She forged on to get her associate's degree, worked as a dietician until she got tired of telling people what and how much to eat, and earned her nursing degree. Mom became a registered nurse, working at the VA hospital, telling old soldiers to take better care of themselves.

She had taken care of Gregory's dad once, making sure he'd eat something before he could have his coffee. He, too, was a World War II veteran.

My mother's tenacity and ability to face and overcome so many obstacles with the strength and fortitude of a soldier *is* why she will always be my hero. *God, I miss her so much!*

***

"Here! Take our picture!" George handed the small box camera to me. After a quick demo, I lifted it, lined my father and husband in the frame, and snapped the picture.

"You need to get one to show the ladies. You might find one who'll want to marry your ugly mug one day," Roderick jested. I smacked Roderick's arm, and he winked at me.

"Or," I interjected, "You may want a photograph to commemorate this moment in life. You can pass it down to your children as proof of the great stories you tell."

George smiled. "I like the way you think, Nora."

George pushed Roderick playfully out of the frame and posed. Instantaneously, my heart stopped for a few beats. I recognized this. I've seen it before. I still had the picture in my photo album, dated to this day. It took a few seconds to calm my jittering nerves as I lifted the camera with shaky hands. My voice rattled as I said to my father, "Say cheese!"

He stood at ease in his smart uniform with his hat tilted in the exact position I remembered. The expression on his face was more of a grimace with the sun in his eyes. And when he looked at the camera, chills passed through me. Because it was like looking at a ghost from the past, but here he was in living flesh.

I snapped the photo before I lost my nerve and heard the click. I knew how the picture would turn out without seeing an instantaneous result, like on a cell phone.

The expression goes, 'A picture is worth a thousand words.' It is a singular memory captured in time. We try to recall everything that happened around that moment, how we felt and lived, and how much we've changed since then. It would haunt me forever, knowing that I was the one who took my father's photo.

Seventy-eight years ago.

FOXTROT

I wanted to recall this entire day with my husband and father in the future. I could almost feel the photograph in my hands. And I knew all the answers to the questions behind it.

We returned to the bar, where George and I helped Roderick finish cleaning and preparing to open later that afternoon. Roderick had cleared some floor space and came to me, holding his hand out.

"Care to cut a rug?" he asked.

George took that as a cue, selected a record, and put it on the player. I felt nervous and hesitant as Roderick led me to the open space. Nora may be a dancer.

I was not.

A familiar song began to play, and my nerves faded as a smile stretched my lips.

"I love this song," I said.

George sang along to the Bing Crosby tune, Accentuate the Positive. He used to sing it to me when I was a child. Back then, I had some clue what the words meant, but the catchy lyrics accompanied by my father's smooth, bass voice always cheered me up. I usually sang it to myself when I was in a good mood.

In retrospect, I should have adopted the song as a personal anthem and sung it as a healing balm to my blues. The words finally held the meaning intended.

Even as a young man, George was perceptive and must have known I needed to "*accentuate the positive and eliminate the negative*" in my life.

Roderick and I moved in step together to the charming, upbeat melody, and I laughed as he lifted me around the waist and spun me. Then he pointed at George, singing, "Don't mess with Mr. In Between."

George lifted his hands in mock defense and said, "I'm not getting in between anybody."

The music changed tempo with brass instruments roaring, transforming the atmosphere with kinetic energy. Roderick and I moved into a swing jump, and jive, and I was astounded at how Nora's muscle memory kicked in and didn't miss a step. I laughed when Roderick spun my body around, and George stepped in to catch me. We immediately upped the pace, and George gave Roderick a challenging grin.

He took my hands, and we jumped in and out, shuffling our feet from side to side. George arched his brow, sticking his tongue out sideways between his lips in concentration, which cracked me up because he looked hilarious. He spun me back to Roderick, and we increased the pace.

Roderick lifted me in the air, and as I sailed up and then downward, I gripped his shoulders as my legs parted and flew around his waist, sticking out straight behind him. From there, he lifted me again, and this time he dropped me lower, where my legs swung straight between his. My feet barely touched the ground as Roderick lifted me again, and I kicked my feet out behind me in a fast cyclic motion.

Roderick set me back on my feet, and we continued to dance like it was nobody's business. George whooped and hollered as he shuffled his feet and danced like he was the cat's meow. Amid it all, I was mystified and mesmerized by the synergistic vibes of our energy. We were like a powerhouse trio of positive exaltations rumbling through the stratosphere. I felt so alive; I thought my soul might burst into sparks of joy rippling and sailing through space and time.

When the music ended, we collapsed to the floor in giddy exhaustion. Roderick was laughing and breathing heavily as my head lay on his outstretched arm.

"I didn't know I could dance like that," I panted.

"*I* didn't know you could dance like that," Roderick laughed and tried to catch his breath.

"I thought I was a dancer," I said as if I wasn't sure.

"You thought you were a dancer?" George asked. "Did you forget you danced? We watched you practice for your performance at the Cincinnati Music Hall a week before we left."

"I performed at the Cincinnati Music Hall?" I asked in disbelief.

"She's a humble gal," George jested. "Did you bump your head, Nora?"

"She did, actually," Roderick intervened. "Last night."

"On the headboard," I said. I slapped my hand over my mouth.

George smiled so big, and my face must have turned ten shades of beetroot as I realized what my words implicated. George laughed, and I shook my head.

"No, no, no! That's not what I meant!" I defended.

George grinned and then looked at me pitifully. “Poor gal! Maybe you should be resting since you probably didn’t sleep much last night.”

“I’m fine,” I protested. “I’ve slept enough these past few years.”

Roderick and George didn’t know I was referring to my future life, where I was so sad and empty that all I felt like doing was lying in bed. I was wide awake, breathing in this life and not wanting to take one minute for granted. I had so much energy coursing through me I could probably dance circles around them into the wee hours of the morning.

“Maybe just a nap. I’ll go with you,” Roderick suggested with a wink.

“I’m not tired.” I folded my arms and pouted. George and Roderick laughed.

“What?” I snapped.

George leaned toward Roderick and whispered in his ear. Roderick smiled and chuckled.

“What are you two conspiring?” I asked.

“Nothing,” Roderick said.

“I’m going to go home and get some rest,” George said. “I’ll see you both tomorrow.”

“You’re leaving?” I whined. *Don’t go now, Daddy!*

“I’m tired. I need to get settled in my new place and take a long nap,” George said. “Will Eugene be here tomorrow?”

“Eugene?” I questioned. I saw George’s confusion and realized that maybe I should take a break and regroup my brain cells. I was slipping and nearly giving the plot away.

“You know what? I think I will take a nap.” I began walking towards the door that led upstairs.

"Eh-hem!" Roderick cleared his throat, and I turned to look at him. He pointed to a door in the opposite direction.

Crap!

I turned and walked in the direction he pointed. I opened the door to a closet with cleaning supplies, cursed under my breath, and closed it. Roderick cleared his throat again and motioned to the next door with his finger. I felt like an imbecile. I took a breath and turned the knob on the next door.

By then, George was laughing his ass off, and Roderick had a huge grin. Roderick approached me, hovering; he leaned in and asked, "Do I need to show you to our room and tuck you in, sweetheart?"

"Do I need to show you to the bathroom so I can help you wash that smug grin off your face?" I asked.

George snickered, and I looked his way and smiled. I knew he approved of my standing up for myself. My father raised my sisters and me to defend ourselves, especially against predators of the testosterone fuel persuasion.

"You need a shower, Roddy," I said, "Because you stink! And I don't just mean your armpits." I stepped into the stairwell and slammed the door in Roderick's face. George's laughter behind the door made me the happiest I'd felt in a long time.

"Ha, ha," Roderick replied with a monotone huff.

My head was still reeling over the fact that I had spent the day with my father. And again, when he told me, I had performed at the Cincinnati Music Hall. It was the same place I attended my mother's college graduation ceremony. I sat on the upper balcony shouting, "***Way to go, Mom***," as she walked across the same stage and received her Associate's Degree in Science—forty-five years into the future.

So many places held echoes from the past. How could one find the epicenter of those echoes? Was it through the soul itself? Or, perhaps, it was through God's voice.

God did work in mysterious ways. And I wondered at the mystery of my presence in this time era. Were we meant to carry the memories from one point of existence to the next? I would not think so in this capacity.

I didn't recall anything before the age of three when I woke into existence one day. It felt like I had forgotten everything that came before. At the same time, I knew I had a connection with the three little girls who chased each other into the room as I lifted my weary head and rubbed my sleepy eyes.

I felt drawn to the young woman with long dark hair and green eyes who smiled lovingly at us as I joined whom I somehow knew to be my sisters in play. I relished in her warm embrace, and the word 'Mommy' left my lips. Everything snapped into place like puzzle pieces as I felt a sense of acceptance. From that moment on, I found peace as I pieced together who I was.

I remembered my dad talking about God, Jesus, the angels, and Heaven. It felt like a seed of truth sprouted inside my little heart but left a question mark lingering. I'd lost a connection, a rift in communication with an old friend who'd shared all their secrets with me. I had to say goodbye to them and forget everything they'd shared for a while. Wiped clean was the slate of memories, and I reawakened into a new consciousness.

In a sense, I felt reassigned to find that connection through the trial and error of my existence.

I recalled my mother telling me, "Life is a test. As long as you keep trying, you will pass."

JULIET

I always believed in putting myself in another's shoes to understand them. As I stood in Nora's shoes rifling through the chifforobe with dresses, blouses, and slacks, I still tried to understand why and how I ended up here. When my consciousness woke last night, I wondered where Nora's mind went.

Since we were of one soul, did it mean we shared the same consciousness? Or was I under some sort of subliminal compulsion where she remained quiet and allowed me to figure it out by myself? Maybe her conscience slumbered in my dormant vessel since our soul was here.

I couldn't begin to comprehend how it all worked. But, seeing how I was still here, for now, I'd try to make the best of my situation. I could appreciate the ease at which Nora's body moved, free of pain, aside from the slight twinge in my head that reminded me of the possibility this was a temporary situation.

I heard the water running through the pipes in the wall and smiled, knowing Roderick had taken my advice to shower. He didn't stink, as I had poked at him in jest, but he was being considerate. And considering we hadn't yet consummated our marriage, I knew he was preparing himself for the possibility. It made me shiver, with heat bubbling through my core. I still felt guilty and selfish at the prospect of taking something that belonged to Nora, a memory that she should make with Roderick.

I wondered if she was there the first time Gregory and I met. Perhaps she had been my tie to the past, like an imaginary friend or a guardian angel sharing all the answers and mysteries I had lost. By Divinity's design, she had to let go, and perhaps it broke her heart as much as it did mine when it was time to move on with my new life. The pain of letting go must have been so prevalent that cleansing the memory of the emotion was necessary so I could discover the joy that awaited.

How far had I fallen that God deemed it necessary to take me on this journey? Alive, but not living. My vessel was lingering in stasis. I had never heard of a soul meeting its mate in a past life while its body remained viable in the future.

The futuristic concept of time travel still consisted of the idea that a physical body traveled back and forth through time. But had the soul already been capable? Was I living proof? Maybe.

Or maybe I *was* dreaming.

I could spin this record backward and forward till the needle wore to a dull nub and never know for sure.

I had removed my dress and bra and put on a nightgown just as Roderick stepped into the room with a towel wrapped around his waist. I bit my lower lip as I eyed his lean muscular torso. I froze when I saw something I hadn't seen before. The shiny pink scar from a bullet wound on his upper left pectoral muscle looked like it had missed his heart by inches.

"You were shot!" I said worriedly.

I approached my husband, and my fingers grazed the scar where the taught flesh looked like it had recently healed. "When did this happen?"

"February 14th, in Italy," Roderick replied.

"You were shot! In the chest! On Valentines Day?" I took a deep breath, trying to ease my astonishment along with the ache in my chest at the thought that he could have died that day.

"Did Nora know?"

"No. I was alive, so I didn't want you to worry. By the time I was out of the hospital, the Germans had surrendered. So, I remained focused on healing and getting my strength back."

"You didn't want ***me*** to worry?"

"Exactly. You said it yourself, Rachael. If I am Gregory, then you are Nora. And I didn't want ***you***, my wife, to worry. My recovery wasn't so bad."

"Roderick! Are you serious? That bullet missed your heart by inches!" I rested my palm over his heart, and he pressed my hand deeper.

"And do you feel that?" He asked. "My heart still beats for you."

I drew in a staggered breath. "Mine too."

I dreamed of a love so true where two hearts beat for one another. I dated a few boys through high school. But that was the problem. They were boys. They were cocky yet unsure of themselves. They wanted to be exclusive, but only for the physical benefits. When it came to emotions of the heart, I felt no connection.

I was still in high school when I saw the news footage of the war in Iraq. Unbeknownst to me, my future husband was fighting in a real war, and recognizing it years later was profound.

In November 1994, I was tired of the internal battle of feeling alone. I had family and friends close by who loved me, but they had their lives to live. It was a crowded loneliness with a void in my heart that needed to be filled. So, one afternoon, I sat on my bed and prayed. I prayed like I had never prayed before in my life.

"Dear God,

I want a good man like my dad. He needs to be a hard worker that takes care of his family. He must be capable of working with his hands to fix things when they break. He loves his parent and treats them with respect. He is honest, trustworthy, responsible, kind, and caring.

He must have a great sense of humor and make me laugh. He needs to be at least as tall as I am and takes care of his body. I want him to have dark hair and blue eyes. He can't be a smoker, an alcoholic, or do drugs. I hate watching sports, so please, he can't be a sports fanatic. He won't cheat on me or break my heart. He believes in the golden rule, fights for what he believes in, and his causes are worthy in your eyes. Most of all, he believes in you. Thank you for my future husband, which you prepare for me. In Jesus' Name, Amen."

***

"How did you and Nora meet?" I asked.

Roderick smiled. "Well, I already told you where we met. Here let me show you something."

He went to a writing desk, where he opened a drawer and pulled out a stack of letters. Sifting through them, he pulled one out, handed it to me, and said, "This is the first letter I wrote after arriving in Italy."

"That is where she kept them," I said. In a desk drawer. How obvious! But how was I to know that? They could've been in a box under the bed or on a closet shelf.

"Nora moved in right after I left. Since we were married, there was no point in paying rent for two places."

"Makes sense," I agreed. Roderick and I exchanged a smile as I opened the envelope.

"Read it aloud," Roderick encouraged, "I want to hear your voice and what you think."

"You do?" I asked.

"Of course I do." He grinned. He waved his encouragement, and I nodded.

"Okay! I usually have to plead for Gregory's attention to read something to him," I cleared my throat.

"Why is that?" Roderick looked perplexed.

"Well, like I mentioned before. We've been married twenty-eight years, and we've both been guilty of rambling on. Our interests have changed somewhat over the years. I enjoy writing, but he's mostly only interested in the juicy parts when I want to read to him."

Roderick chuckled. "I see what you mean now when you say he's a horn dog."

I laughed. "Any opportunity he gets to play the part. He's ready and willing."

"I can't fault him." Roderick smiled. "So, why don't you read to me, darling? I'd love to hear what makes him ready and willing."

I giggled as my belly stirred with warmth. "Okay then…" I looked at the letter. "You're penmanship is nice."

"Is that your way of saying it's at least legible?"

"Well, if I can read it without squinting and sounding out the words phonetically, then yes."

"Okay, go ahead." He gestured.

I smiled and nodded.

"October 22, 1943.

My Dearest Nora,

We've arrived in Italy, and these first few days have been hard. I'm struggling to stay awake after the long stretch here. Thank goodness for coffee. It tastes like bitter tar, but it does the job.

What is even more bitter is the feeling of missing you. To find the sweetness, I replay the memory of the first time we met. I never had the chance to tell you, but my plans for that day nearly took me in the opposite direction. I must confess I was trying to find some company before I had to leave for war. I was lonely and knew being in a stranger's arms was a temporary remedy.

Believe it or not, it was George who suggested we go to the diner to grab a coffee and think about our life choices. I called him a stick in the mud. But he warned me to be careful where I stuck my stick because I didn't want to go to war with a case of something clapping in my pants."

A laugh caught in my throat, and I had to pause my reading. "My dad was your Jiminy Cricket?"

Roderick laughed. "It sounds strange. But for some reason, that day, he acted out of character. Perhaps the impending dark cloud that hung over our heads made him stand on the side of caution."

"Or, maybe he knew. Like intuition. He was a steward of caution and sensibility when it came to my sisters and me. He always told us to listen to our inner voices to avoid danger."

"And I'm sure being a soldier, and fatherhood had much to do with that," Roderick added.

"I would agree with that. Being a soldier's wife and a mother has a way of sharpening one's senses." I looked at the letter. "Shall I continue?"

"Read on," Roderick encouraged.

I lifted the page and harrumphed.

"As fate would have it, a beautiful angel entered the diner. With strawberry blond hair, green eyes, and a face that Heaven kissed with a sheen of loveliness. The sight of her held me captivated.

And when she looked my way and smiled, I nearly spilled my coffee. She sat at the booth behind ours, and luckily, George didn't see her first. I told him my destiny just walked through the door, and he couldn't steal it from me.

She kept giving me her eyes. I felt it each time before she did. Because I made sure she saw me looking back at her every time. George excused himself to the men's room only to get a chance to see what I saw. He saw her alright! When he sat back down, he said, "You lucky S.O.B. Go talk to her before she gets away."

I was trying to keep my cool, but I was sweating like a pig, and I knew my armpits would give away my nervousness. I almost let her get away. She paid for her coffee and rose from the table.

"She's leaving, you idiot!" George whispered.

Panic set in at the thought of never seeing her again. I flinched as she turned to head out the door. But then she paused, turned around, and went to the ladies' room. I couldn't follow her, so I waited, with my knees jitterbugging beneath the table. She came out and nearly passed again when George, my hero, said, "Excuse me, miss! Your shoe is untied."

She thanked him and looked down. She was wearing ballet flats, and her face turned as strawberry as her hair. Before I lost my nerve, I told her not to mind, my friend. From there, I told her my name and asked if she wanted to go to the USO dance with me. She looked like a dancer—a lovely ballerina.

Like a fine lady, she responded, "My name is Nora, and I'd love to go to the dance with you."

My heart soared as she accepted my invitation, and we ended up leaving the diner together. It was the best day of my life, meeting her. I loved her the first moment I saw her.

You. My Nora.

I love you still. And I will love you always.

Yours truly,

Roderick"

I held the letter to my chest and sighed. "That was romantic, the way you referred to Nora as an angel and spoke of her in the third person. I can't believe my dad was there playing matchmaker."

"How did you and Gregory meet?" Roderick asked.

"Believe it or not, we met at a Mexican fast-food restaurant on Grand Avenue. My best friend in high school, Marissa, was in a relationship with Gregory's little brother, Johnathan. But I never knew Gregory existed until the day we met."

"Really? Did your eleven-year age difference have anything to do with it?"

"Partly. Johnathan just never mentioned him before. We were Sophomores when Gregory was fighting in the Middle East."

"Another war?" Roderick questioned.

"There are several more conflicts between now and our time in the future."

Roderick looked at the ceiling and said, "I wonder if I'll punch my ticket to the Hereafter in the next?"

"Don't say that, Roderick. I need you. Nora needs you!"

Roderick looked at me empathetically. "I'm sorry, Rachael. That was insensitive of me. It's a soldier's mentality. The thought crossed my mind every day during the war."

"No, I'm sorry. I get it. It's just hard knowing it is a possibility. I spent my whole life waiting for my soulmate and came to find out he was a soldier. It's a high-risk job that takes courage and conviction to stand and fight. To be the person waiting on the other side is its own kind of battle. When we lose our loved ones in the fray, we lose everything that matters."

"I knew I was adding a heavy weight to your shoulders by asking you to be my wife. Your courage and sacrifice mean so much to me. Just as much as I'm sure that in our future life, Gregory feels the same."

"He does," I replied. "We're a team."

Roderick leaned forward to press his forehead to mine. "We are."

INDIA

Gregory and I were obsessed with one another during our first year of marriage. We lived in family housing in Ft. Knox and could still drive up every other weekend to visit family and friends. We lived each day wrapped up in each other's arms, every free moment we had together. We lived and loved like tomorrow might never come.

I thought I had what it took to be a young Army wife. Gregory had already served thirteen years before we met. He had been to Germany, Texas, Iraq, and Germany again before returning to Ft. Knox. The timing was kismet.

Still, I was foolish for thinking, '*What could possibly happen in the next seven to ten before he retired?*'

I was no Nostradamus. And I still operated under the impression that there was nothing to worry about if the conflict wasn't knocking at my door. That was my pre-Army wife mentality. Ignorance, arrogance, and denial were my go-to to keep my mental checks and balances. It was only a matter of time before Gregory would receive orders to deploy. That first year was a blessed reprieve from reality. We lived in a bubble of bliss.

That was until the day he came home and made an announcement which shook me.

Sitting outside enjoying the lovely springtime Kentucky weather, I smiled at Gregory as he exited the car. He stood in the street and looked up at me. "I have some news, and it is good or bad, depending on how you want to look at it."

"What is it?" I asked. Anxiety rose in my chest. It arrived, the day that proverbial pin would burst our little bubble.

"We're PCSing to Texas."

My eyes nearly popped out of my head. "TEXAS?" I gasped.

"Texas," Gregory repeated.

I'd never been far away from home. I never considered that I would live anywhere else outside of the Tri-State. Ohio, Kentucky, and Indiana. That was it!

I knew I couldn't argue against it. Staying in Kentucky or Ohio and finding a place close to family wasn't an option. I married a traveling soldier. Moving was an inevitable part of the package. But TEXAS! It may as well have been India, as far and as foreign to me as I imagined. Wasn't it all desert, tumbleweeds, and cowboys riding horses on ranches, plowing farmland and oilfields? And it was hot! I didn't like hot. It got hot in the summertime in Kentucky but didn't stay hot.

Being away from my family tested my resolve. But I loved Gregory so much; I was willing and ready to follow him anywhere.

We'd weather each storm together like in the Tanya Tucker song, 'Two Sparrows In A Hurricane.' We were *"Trying to find our way. With a head full of dreams and faith that could move anything."*

I wasn't sure my faith was strong enough to move anything. I did have a 'head full of dreams.' That was for sure. It was us against the world, and love was the determining factor as to whether or not we could make it uphill.

***

I felt like I was chipping away in a dark tunnel. Slowly, the grains of earth crumbled, and the mechanical beeping of a steady pulse sounded from somewhere in the distance, and as it came closer, I could hear my heartbeat drumming within my ears. The feel of my chest rising and falling accommodated the sound of my breaths.

Gregory's voice pleaded, "Don't you dare give up, Rachael! We are a team! Our children need you! I need you!"

I'm here! I couldn't move my mouth. My lips were dry and sealed together. My tongue felt parched and resistant to movement, and my eyelids felt like rough sandpaper against my corneas, incapable of opening as they felt glued shut.

I felt my soul drifting in-between time and space. A tugging pulled me back and forth, and I felt like I was in the valley of shadows between two enormous mountains, not knowing which way to turn. There was stillness there. It was peaceful.

In the distance, I saw a man dressed in long robes. He lifted a staff. It had a crook on the end. He pointed it at me and turned toward the mountain in the east, where the sun began cresting over the peak. He pointed to the mountain and said, "Follow the light."

I looked toward the mountain, and the rays of the sun were so bright I had to cast my eyes toward the earth. And I saw my shadow stretch far across the valley where it touched the base of the next mountain.

As if not knowing the path of the sun, I asked, "Which way does it go?"

"To the crossroads," He answered.

"And where do I go from there?"

"Home!" The man's form faded till he was no more.

Home!

The word has multiple meanings. It was a physical dwelling. A place where a family lived. And a place where we're meant to feel safe. It was the hearts' anchor point, where we lived and loved. It was a place of rest and a final destination after a long road traveled.

I longed to go home. But which home? I stood at the crossroads, feeling pulled in every direction. But one direction pulled me more so than the rest. It was a force so magnetic, like the draw of a compass needle pointing the way north. So, I began walking in that direction. The farther I walked, the more I felt a power greater than any other.

It was the power of love.

TANGO

Surrounded in silence, I could hear his breaths. We kept each other warm beneath the sheets long after the music ended and the candles had burned themselves out. I opened my eyes in the early morning hours and saw him staring back at me.

"You are so beautiful." Gregory moved his fingertips up and down my back.

"Will you still love me when I'm old, wrinkled, and grey?" I asked.

Gregory smiled. "I'll be chasing you around the house till the day we die."

I knew I would marry Gregory even before the first time we made love. He'd already shown me the man he was. His honor and dedication had already made him the *Hero of My Heart*. It was only a matter of time before we said, I do.

The night before, I prepared myself for the possibility of our intimate unification. Wearing only a robe, I appreciated Gregory's masculine form as he came into the room wearing only a towel around his waist. A selection of romantic melodies played on his stereo, and candles lit the room in a complimentary ambiance.

Gregory's lips brushed my forehead. He took my face in his hands and kissed my cheek, then moved to my lips. I melted into our kiss, we moved languidly, and my lips became pliable as he slid his tongue inside my mouth. I moaned at the feeling and taste of him.

The heat of our desire pulsated at the surface as I allowed Gregory the pull the tie of my robe. It opened, exposing the midline of my body, revealing the inner curves of my breasts down my belly button to my pelvis.

My legs began shaking as Gregory's fingers traced the line of my lips, down my chin, neck, and between the swells of my breasts. My breath hitched as he lingered there, momentarily skimming his fingertips left and right, not going beyond where the robe draped over the rest of my flesh.

His fingertips against my abdomen felt ticklish, and my stomach dipped inward as he continued down. He traced my belly button, circling it with his thumb, and my breaths doubled as he approached the apex between my legs. Again, he stopped, and his fingers played at the elastic band of my panties. He pulled the band slightly away from my stomach before letting them snap back against my skin.

I gasped as I clung to his shoulders in a solid grip, afraid my legs would give, and I'd collapse to the floor. His kissable lips curved into a delectable smile, and the muscles in his jaw twitched. He licked his lips like he was savoring an exquisite dessert. It was so sexy that the heat inside intensified, and I almost came undone.

He fixated on my body as he took his time revealing it piece by piece. I moaned, and Gregory's blue eyes flew up to meet mine. As the words to Eternal Flame played, Gregory kissed me, then, with a pleading breath, he said, "I want to make love to you."

His words sent me to the edge, and I was already tipping toward the abyss of our passion. The apex between my legs throbbed madly, and desire rushed like hot currents, making me ache for his touch.

I couldn't hold back a moment longer. My hands took hold of my future, pulled it toward me, and our kiss blazed like the rays of the midday August sun. Gregory pulled desperately at the lapel of my robe, and I moved my arms to allow it to fall free from my body. All that separated us now were my panties and the towel around his waist. He backed me to the wall, pressing his body flush with mine.

I could feel him against me, filled and firm.

Gregory broke our kiss and asked, "Are you ready?"

I was panting. "Yes. I need you. I need you now!"

With my back pressed against the wall, Gregory kissed a path down my body. He came to a squat, looking up at me as he curled his thumbs into my waistband. My heart hammered in my chest as I looked at his hooded eyes and nodded. He freed me from my last covering with the slide of his fingers over my hips, thighs, and legs. His hands ran smoothly up my curves as he stood, and I pulled his towel free.

I couldn't wait a moment longer as I threw my arms around Gregory's neck, and he pulled my body to him, closing the distance between us. Our lips collided, and I felt my womanhood swelling and blooming like a wild orchid drenched in sweet morning dew heated by the rays of the warm risen sun.

Gregory laid me on the bed, and we became one flesh as our bodies and souls combined and melded into one another. The initial burning stretch subsided with the momentary pain, replaced by the pleasure of being filled and complete.

I received my life mate fully with all the love in my heart and soul, and together we soared on eagles' wings till we touched the heavens. Our wing tips kissed the sky, our talons locked, and we tumbled in a dizzying spiral, unable to let go for fear of truly falling, one without the other.

And as we came down from our high, I saw Gregory looking back at me with no hint of doubt in his eyes.

“I love you, Rachael.”

“I love you, Gregory.”

***

Roderick was looking at me when I opened my eyes. His fingers tips brushed a lock of my hair from my forehead down, and he tucked it behind my ear.

“It sounded like you had a nice dream.” He smiled.

I was happy to see him, but I felt confused, because didn’t I leave? I thought I’d traveled somewhere. I felt tired like I had gone on a long walk. Then I was home in Gregory’s arms. We were young again and experienced our first-time together.

I yawned and stretched, feeling Nora’s muscles flex without all of the creaking and popping I usually experienced. It was rather refreshing. Roderick’s eyes were on me, trailing along my curves; that devilish grin told me how much he appreciated the sight.

He wasn’t bad to look at himself, my husband, a young fit soldier, returned home from war. His blue eyes penetrated mine as he held my gaze, still looking to see that I was there. Or was he looking for Nora? Perhaps both.

As if knowing what I was thinking, he said, “I see you and her. I see the love you have for me. Is it different?”

"Is what different?" I asked.

He leaned in and pressed his lips to mine. It was sweet, tender, and non-intrusive. Thankfully he didn't press for more. I had a thing about morning breath.

He backed away and searched again; those blue pools shifted from side to side. "How does it feel being with me? In this life?"

"The physical difference is fascinating, exhilarating. We're both young again. I can't pretend that it doesn't *do* something. It makes me nervous and excited but also cautious and guarded," I admitted.

Roderick's brows knitted. "How so?"

"Well, I'm in Nora's body. We're the same soul but not the same consciousness, yet I still feel connected with you as my husband as much as Gregory. But if we were to go further, I feel like I'd be stealing something, a special moment."

"I don't see how. I think it would be more like sharing something phenomenal, an opportunity unheard of. Who gets a chance to experience what we are, Rachael? It's a once-in-a-billion lifetime chance."

"But I don't know why or how it happened. Getting to see my dad again was cathartic. The pain of missing him is gone, and I know he is in God's hands. But when it comes to us, I still feel like there's some resistance, and it's within me. It's something I'm struggling to release. And I know I must let it go before I can claim peace within my soul."

"You're at a crossroads, Rachael. It's your decision to make. I'll help you in any way I can. But I can't decide for you."

"In a way, I know what's weighing on me, but I don't know how to give it up. It's an emotional crutch that serves my selfishness."

"Selfishness?" Roderick sat up in bed with a look of disbelief. "How can someone who's dedicated their life to another, leaving behind everything she holds dear to follow the man she loves into battle, who birthed and raised three children, claim to be selfish?"

"You're a soldier. You know about logistics, Roderick. There's always a need for a battle plan. The enemy can find breaches in the line of defense. He comes like a thief in the night, slipping in through the shadows. He knows our weaknesses and breaks our defenses down from within."

"He's also a liar, Rachael."

"I know!" I shook my head, feeling those lies beat around the fortress of my mind. "And in a way, I've allowed myself to fall dependent. It's a pitiful excuse to dismiss myself from living in the light. I love and crave the light, but I lean weary in the darkness. It's a battle I feel I can't win alone."

Roderick pulled me to him. "Rachael, you're hiding from the truth. But you're not alone. No one can wage war against themselves without some outside force breaking down their strongholds. And no one can fight those battles relying on their strength alone."

"I know this too!" I cried. "I've tried, and I've prayed to God to take this heavy yolk off my shoulders. Something inside me keeps wanting to put it back on like if others see it, they'll feel sympathy for my plight and ease off on expecting much from me. I'm exhausted from giving pieces of myself to others who rely on me, and I'm tired of the rejections I've received from those who do not matter. I've wanted more than this identity, and I've grown complacent, accepting that there's no chance of accomplishing my dreams."

"What are your dreams, Rachael?"

"I want to be seen, but not to the point that it smothers me. I want my work to be recognized and appreciated. I want my dreams to be read by the masses and success to come in a way that could provide for our family, and you, Gregory, could finally take a break. You gave so much of yourself, and that's what I meant when I said I was selfish because I stood by and allowed you to toe the line. You worked and provided, took care of the finances, helped around the house, fixed everything, changed dirty diapers, and made sure we were well-fed. And I fell complacent in allowing you to do it all."

Roderick turned me to face him. He lifted my chin so I was looking him in the eyes. The look he gave commandeered my full attention. "Sharing a life doesn't mean it's 50/50 all the time. We are two halves of one whole, and sometimes the scales tip. You said we are a team, but you discredit yourself. And when you discredit yourself, you discredit me as well. Do you think of me so lowly?"

My mouth opened and closed. I swallowed a lump, then opened it again. "I. I never thought of it that way. I. I'm sorry."

"Never say you're sorry, Rachael. Admit you realize it's not just you who has flaws. Find and acknowledge your strengths. You've contributed how you can and the best you can. Am I so dense-headed in our next life that I've not recognized and explained it to you?"

"You're an intelligent man, but the life you endured in your past made you more reserved. You're very loving and caring but less expressive when discussing emotions. I've never faulted you for that."

"It seems you fault me far less than you do yourself. It must be overwhelming taking on every emotion and caring so deeply for the people around you," Roderick said tenderly.

"I do care. Very much. About everything and everybody. I just don't care enough about myself," I admitted.

"How can you, when you're so depleted? I know how that feels, darling! The battlefield takes a heavy toll on your emotions. Your battle is here!" Roderick tapped the side of his head. "It's a location you can't escape because it's a part of you. It goes where you go. Sees what you see, and it takes your mind hostage. You have to decide whether or not to set it free."

“You are an amazing man, Roderick Gregory Akner. Are you some sort of Freudian savant?”

Roderick laughed. “No. I don’t think so. My uncle Eugene, believe it or not, is quite attuned to the psychology of human nature. He’s been a moonshiner and bartender most of his adult working life. I spent some time listening in on his sage advice.”

“That must be why some people drink away their worries. It comes with free advice from sensible people,” I surmised.

“It’s also why people make toasts to the good memories.” Roderick climbed out of bed and went to a cabinet, where he pulled out a bottle and glasses. He poured a warm amber liquid into them and carried them over, handing one to me. “I’d like to propose a toast.”

“A drink? This early in the morning? I’m not a drinker, you know.”

“It’s not about the drink, Rachael. It’s about commemorating a memory. Do you want to make a toast or not, sweetheart?”

“It couldn’t hurt, I suppose. What are we making a toast to today?”

“Now that’s a good idea,” Roderick said as if agreeing to a proposal.

“What idea?” I asked.

“Every day, we make a toast to something. It doesn’t have to be with alcohol, just whatever we start our day with.” Roderick lifted his glass. “Here’s to you, my wife. My equal. My everything. Without you, I’d be a lonely, miserable man, a good-for-nothing bum! We will remain champions lifting each other when the scales tip too low. Our love for one another will keep the balance so the scales never crash.

He held his glass toward me, and I smiled, clinking mine to his; I said, “To love in good measure.”

Roderick smiled brightly, "Pressed down, shaken, and running over." He tilted his glass to his lips, took a hearty swallow, and I tipped my glass to take a small sip. The alcohol burned my tongue and throat, and I coughed.

"Perhaps wine next time," I suggested.

"Sounds like a romantic date. Tonight Mrs. Akner?"

"For you, Mr. Akner. I'm available."

I pondered on Roderick's words and realized my misgivings. I always held my husband in high regard. I never thought I had discredited him. But what Roderick said made sense. Gregory conducted himself by a moral code of honor. He had a leadership role in his job and our marriage. He never let the circumstances of his upbringing and unstable environment dictate his character. He vowed to break the pattern of abuse which his mother and siblings suffered at the hands of their father. And no matter how upset he'd get, he never raised a hand to me. He scarcely raised his voice, for that matter.

My mother warned me to steer clear of any man who drinks too much. Gregory used to drink and party in his younger years, but he quit when he made a vow to God to live better. And by the time we'd met, he was a new man, a man prepared by God to become the husband I had prayed for.

WHISKEY

I took a moment to read one of Nora's letters. I noticed the post date of one, which fell on my mother's birthday eleven years before she was born. I pulled it from its envelope.

"March 27th, 1944

My Dearest Roddy,"

There was an accident at the bar the other day. Don't worry. Everyone is fine. I threw a shoe at Eugene's head when I kicked too hard during my cabaret dance. The comedic timing had a few people rolling in their seats, and they said he may have well deserved it too. But lucky for him, he ducked when my shoe flipped off my foot and sailed over his head. He told me kicking around like a showgirl might not be the best dance for the audience.

I promised to tighten the buckles on my straps so I wouldn't kick them off during my performance. Eugene threatened to dock my pay if I lost a shoe again, even during practice.

I told him that if he did that, I would throw every shoe I owned at him. Then he said I would never get my shoes back, and he'd still cut my pay. I told him I would do a barefoot victory dance while I passed out his precious Columbian cigars to every chap who came through the door. The very idea made him angry. But guess what he did? Eugene bought the cheapest cigars he could find and told me I could stand outside, tap dance, and sell them for a quarter over cost to all the Joes coming into the bar.

The nerve of him to say it was all his idea! I was miffed. So I refused. He promised to cut me a higher percentage in tips instead of docking my pay. Your uncle is a real pain in my keester. I guess I should be thankful he returned to keep the place running while you are away. Heaven knows this is not my specialty. But I'm grateful for a paying job since dance gigs are getting harder to come by around here. I'd never be a Vegas type of showgirl. I'd have to travel otherwise, and I'm staying put till you get home. I can't wait till you get home!

All my love,

Nora.

I looked at Roderick. "Your uncle Eugene took care of things while you were gone. Did the bar used to belong to him?"

"It still does. It belongs to all of us. He added my name to the deed, so when he dies, there's no fuss," Roderick explained. "He always believed I would return alive, and I was the only person he trusted."

"I can see why." I chuckled as a memory came forth.

"Why would you say that and laugh?" Roderick asked.

"Oh no. It's not you. I was remembering the time I threw my shoe in the Mississippi mud?"

"Mississippi?" Roderick laughed. "Oh. I need to hear this!"

I began telling Roderick the story, and my mind returned to the memory—a memory from the future.

Gregory and I had PCS'd to Camp Shelby in Hattiesburg, Mississippi, in 1999, and one swelting summer day; I tagged along as he mapped a six-mile course through the woods and adjoining field for a training exercise. Gregory plotted the course, and I assisted in sticking flags into the ground. It was humid, having rained heavily the night before, which made the task of pushing the wired markers into the ground easy.

We had reached a point where the ground was muddy, and Gregory stepped through it. I followed, making it two steps, when I felt the gripping suction of the mud encasing my shoe. I struggled to free my foot, and Gregory came to my aid. We wiggled my foot free sans one sneaker, and I had to hop on my other foot to avoid plunging my socked one into the sloppy terrain.

Gregory laughed his ass off as I cried, "Are you going to help me, you big jerk?"

But then I began laughing too as he made of production of freeing my shoe from the mud, wiping it in the grass, and presenting it to me on bended knee like some smartass Prince Charming.

The long trek had nearly worn us out when we got home. But we had so much fun and still enough energy that it carried over to the shower and bedroom. The tightness in my muscles worked to our advantage, as the building pleasure of bodies moving together had me pleading for Gregory never to stop.

The memory of that moment was so sublime I drew upon it as the true-to-life fantasy fuel it was to keep my garden well-tended. And Gregory was a keen gardener. We'd shared a handful of passionate moments I noted in my memory banks on which I drew to keep our sexual encounters lively. We were wild and spry in the season of our youth. Our honeymoon phase lasted the first seven years then things changed.

"What changed?" Roderick asked.

"Everything. When we became parents, I faulted Gregory immensely when I labored and pushed for four hours to give birth to Benjamin. Our son had a big head."

Roderick laughed. "I see. Your body changed. That's a lot for a woman to go through. Was Gregory there for the birth?"

"It was his 39th birthday. So guess what he got for his present that year?" I grinned. "He said when our son was born, he gave up his birthday rights."

"Was he retired from the Army by then?"

"Funny you ask. Gregory missed his Hail and Farewell party on the same day. I heard him tell his commander on the phone that he was sorry he couldn't attend. Something important came up."

"Family is important," Roderick said. "I can't wait till we start ours."

"Well, you know what that requires," I said playfully.

Roderick grinned unabashedly. "Would you like to share with the rest of the class, Mrs. Akner? I'd love to hear more of your birds and bees stories."

I bit my lips. "Perhaps I've overshared already."

"No. Tell me," Roderick insisted. I couldn't deny my husband. Sharing the juicy tidbits with him felt scandalous, but he was still my soulmate.

"Fine!" I huffed. "One day, Gregory and I were riding our bikes home from visiting a friend's house on base. We'd had a great time barbequing and playing games. Midway home, rain began pouring. Thankfully it was summertime, so the cool water falling on our hot skin felt amazing. But soaked-through denim isn't very comfortable. The need to get out of our clothes as soon as we entered the kitchen turned into a fun game of jumping, tripping, and laughing while we peeled each other's clothes off like a second skin. By the time we got down to our underwear, things had gotten pretty hot in the kitchen, if you catch my drift."

I nervously laughed as Roderick licked his lips like he was tasting the moment.

"What else," he asked huskily.

I gulped. "Uhm! Well! After Gregory returned home from his deployment to Bosnia, the soldiers were told not to attempt to woo their spouses right away. Their commanders mentioned something about valuing your spouse and getting reacquainted slowly or some dumb crap like that: but I wasn't having any of that nonsense. I missed our physical connection just as much as everything else. And I made it clear to Gregory on the car ride home that I wasn't willing to wait. I valued him. But I wanted his hands and sexy body all over mine."

Roderick laughed. "That was very forward of you, wife. So, was it different after being apart for so long?" He toyed with the hem of my gown, skimming my thigh with his fingers, and my stomach fluttered.

"It was," I admitted. "Depression had hammered its first heavy blow while Gregory was gone, and I had to force myself out of the house to keep it from latching on and keeping me locked down. So I exercised and took a few classes at the community college. It paid off. I lost a few pounds and kept my mind engaged. And the first moment Gregory and I made it home, we fell into each other's arms. Our physical connection was mind-blowing. It was like riding on a continuous wave of intense pleasure the whole time."

"Rachael?" Roderick said my name breathlessly.

I began to tremble. "Yes, Roderick?"

"The sadness you felt is why we need to be together. We are not ourselves when we're apart. You are my wife. I am your husband. Your voice and those sensual memories have me on the verge of losing my mind. I need you! Not just your body but all of you. We're here together right now in this life. What you and Gregory have shared is beautiful. I want that with you too."

"But, Nora!"

"Is here!" Roderick took my hand and led me to a mirror. "Look closer." He pointed, and I saw her light flash within our shared eyes and gasped in amazement.

I'm here; Nora's voice sounded in my head. Hearing her speak had me at a loss for words momentarily.

"But this is your moment," I sounded hesitant because I wanted it too. My words did not deter Nora as she replied,

And by Our Father's appointing, you're here as well. Like Rachel, you are our soul revival as second and favored by our soul mate. You are here to share in the beauty of this moment so you can see, feel, and know the purity of the love God designed for two meant to be together. We need our husbands. They need us. It is okay. We are the same: Roderick's and Gregory's.

The tears springing forth from Nora's eyes had welled from my emotions. Roderick stood behind me with his hands on my shoulders.

"Miraculous!" He exclaimed, "Home. I see my home in your eyes."

I turned to Roderick, and his soul light flashed from within his eyes.

My lips trembled. "I see mine too. In yours."

Roderick took hold of my shaking hands, kissed them, and pressed them below the scar on his chest, where I could feel his heart beating madly.

"Do you see it now, darling? Love is the victor in all battles! It will always lead us home. Live, Rachael! Love yourself as much as our children love you, as much as I love you. And, most of all, love yourself the way God loves you! Your love was enough for me to survive a bullet to the chest. This moment was God's plan all along! You had to see it to believe it. The scars on our bodies and our minds tell a story but do not dictate our self-worth. Our faith does that!

And Jesus, who took all our sins along with our scars, didn't die on that cross so we could live our lives ashamed of ourselves. He did it so we could see our Father's love. The Father's love is all-encompassing and is meant to build us up.

Don't look in the mirror and allow the enemy to tear you down with lies, Rachael. You've been through your battles, and you are still healing. Claim the shape of your body and all it has endured. The hardship of life and life-giving are gifts meant to strengthen our resolve. Don't you dare give up! Give your sorrows to HIM who loves you, and let Him lift you from the darkness and bring you back into the light!"

The wall in my mind fragmented into a million pieces as I broke down and cried in Roderick's arms. He was my angel sent to reveal the truth. I had a moment with my daddy, and spending a day with him was such a beautiful blessing. But, at this moment, I knew it would be the last till my time came to go home.

It wasn't my time yet, I realized.

Roderick pulled me close and kissed me, and I felt her. Nora's consciousness pressed into the forefront of my mind. Our mind!

"She's here!" I said with complete certainty.

Roderick looked into my eyes. "I know!"

"I love you, Roddy!" The words left my lips, and I felt them too. It was also Nora's moment of confession. And the moment turned to one of passion, and Roderick kissed her. I felt the intensity of the fire, and it made me reach beyond the realm of every inexplicable possibility.

I had thought this moment should be theirs and theirs alone, but my consciousness remained. I recognized the purpose behind everything as I felt the intimacy Roderick and Nora shared. It was no imposition as my husband, and I kissed, touched, and made love for the first time. It was all about love and how to give it, receive it, and accept it in its entirety.

I saw the life they would share. And it was beautiful. It had meaning. And it was worth it. **All of it!**

ECHO

I closed my eyes and relaxed into a memory where my body lay submerged in a tub of steaming hot water. It soothed and loosened my muscles. I knew I had been there too long when my head felt woozy. I leaned forward, pulled the drain plug, and pushed myself to stand. The dizziness intensified, and I leaned against the shower wall. The curtain drew back, and Gregory smiled at me.

“Mind if I join you in the shower?” he asked.

I observed the crochet blanket his mother had made lying on the floor behind him where I had left it. The room was spinning, but I couldn’t help but smile at him. I nodded, and he stepped into the tub and started the shower. Steaming hot water ran into the draining hot water, still ankle-deep around our feet. He pulled me in, kissed me, and looked concerned as my body became listless.

“Are you okay?” he asked.

“I’m hot; the shower is too hot.”

“Oh, I’ll cool it down.” He turned to adjust the taps. Then I heard Gregory’s frightened voice yell, “OH NO,” as I slid sideways against the wall. He reached out to catch me, but it was too late.

I fell from the bathtub and crashed, hitting my head on the floor. Pitch black flickered across my vision, and snippets of my life flashed before me. When I regained consciousness a few moments later, Gregory knelt beside me, looking frightened.

“Rachael!” His voice panicked, “Are you okay?”

My throbbed head, and the corner of the crochet blanket beneath it, only provided a minimal cushion between my skull and the hard-tiled floor. Something in my mind told me it could have been worse if it had not been there.

“I’m going to be sick.” Nausea rolled through me as Gregory helped me sit up. Thankfully the toilet was a foot away. I gripped the bowl and vomited. Gregory held my wet hair to the side, and I thought death might be a better alternative to how I felt.

“I need to take you to the hospital. You may have a concussion.”

“No. I don’t want to go.” I was too stubborn to let him take me. I didn’t want to be separated. Our weekends were too short, and I wanted to spend every second with him. I just needed to lay in bed and let the queasiness subside.

So once more, I closed my eyes and faded into darkness.

There was that strange beeping sound again. I drew a deep breath through my nostrils, and my eyelids cracked open. Everything in me ached. I moaned, and a face I recognized appeared before me.

"Mama?" Sarah asked.

I had trouble parting my lips to respond, so I groaned.

"She's awake!" Sarah cried.

And there he was! My husband, my soul mate, my Gregory!

"Rachael!" He took my hand and wept.

With collective gasps of "MOM," my children came to me, kissing my forehead, hugging me, and crying.

I looked at my surroundings and realized I was in a hospital. I managed to sign my need for water, and my husband nodded. He pressed the button to alert the nursing staff and told them I was awake. The doctor came to talk to me not long after that.

"Mrs. Talbert, you had a hemorrhagic stroke caused by a rupture in an artery on the right side of your brain. Your husband called an ambulance when you struggled to speak, and they got you here in the nick of time. We managed to repair the artery and control the bleeding. You were in a coma for three days. Your waking so soon is miraculous. We will continue to monitor and treat you, and you will remain here as you recover. It may be a week at the minimum before you can return home."

Home! I was home with my family in this beautiful life I would no longer take for granted.

Over the next several days, I understood what I must do to continue to survive. Survival alone was not enough. I needed to live again! And for that, I would have to make significant changes.

I was no longer a spring chicken, as the saying goes. It became a repetitive mantra as I spoke with my sisters on the phone. I adopted a healthier lifestyle which included taking better care of my body and mental health, and Gregory was there for me as I worked harder than before to be there for him and our family.

One year later, I caught the bug of shopping for antiquities at estate sales. When I saw the picture of a tigerwood writing desk, I thought it was a deal at 75 dollars.

"The sales lady said the side drawers were stuck, and there wasn't a key to open the top. So whatever is jamming the drawer is ours to keep," I said.

"It would be cool in it was some World War II memorabilia," Gregory said.

"It's a possibility. The family who owned it said their dad was a WWII veteran. He passed away in the early 1960s."

When we lifted the desk and lay it on its back to slide into our vehicle, I heard the slide and clunk sound from within the bottom drawer. It sounded solid, and I pictured a box of some sort.

"What's this?" Gregory asked. He retrieved a small metal object that had fallen on the ground.

"Oh, cool! That might be the key!" I said.

"We'll open it in the garage when we get home to check for unwanted houseguests," Gregory said.

I nodded in agreement. I loved cleaning and restoring old furniture. It was my next favorite hobby aside from writing. I dusted and applied linseed oil to the tigerwood, polishing it to bring out the natural beauty of its striped duotones. I wanted a small wooden desk to sit at when I wrote. Something about this particular desk made me feel reminiscent.

I had a dream that felt so real; I swore I had lived it. I traced the bits and pieces that remained scattered like breadcrumbs along a path of my memory. It happened when I was in the hospital a year ago. The emotions it evoked were peace, joy, and love. I often pondered on what remained. It was a fine thread that held a strong connection from here to the past.

The vivid color and the sound of the music of a bygone era inspired me. Somedays, I felt my feet moving of their own volition, tapping to the music. Blue eyes filled with love and adoration caused me to pause as my heart might grow wings and fly free from my chest.

My dad's presence wrapped around me with reassuring warmth like a soft tartan blanket filling me with happiness and peace.

I removed a picture of him from my photo album. He looked so handsome in his uniform, with his hat slightly tilted. His casual stance with his hands in his pockets and his squinting eyes caused by the sun shining on his face did not deter the sense of accomplishment in knowing he had served his country.

A handwritten date, August 16, 1945, was on the back of the picture. I didn't know why, but somehow, I felt like some part of that day belonged to me. I didn't recall having this feeling before. It felt like a soul-deep connection.

I should have been born in that era. I was a soldier's wife.

Perhaps I had been. I'll never know for sure.

I put my father's picture in a frame and hung it on my living room wall with the many family members who had served, including my husband and his dad, my sister, brother-in-law, stepbrother, a great uncle, and a nephew.

I missed my dad. That feeling wouldn't ever go away. Remembering was how it was supposed to be. He will always be in my heart for all the days of my life. As long as I lived, he lived.

The lock clicked as I turned the key in the desk drawer. The top drawer had a book which I opened. It was a diary. The dates at the tops of its pages ranged from the 1940s to the '60s. The handwriting was illegible in some places. It reminded me of my mother's 'chicken scratch' as she so joked. The entries were random dates, not day-to-day accounts—sporadic memories which jumped in increments of months to years.

I set it aside and pulled on the knob of the lower drawer. It was stuck tight, so I removed the upper drawer and saw a picture frame tilted sideways. On top of a shoe box, it had caused the drawer to stick. I had to wiggle the edge till it popped free. Then I was able to open the lower drawer.

"A marriage certificate! Why would someone discard a piece of family history this way?" Wondering whom it belonged to and if I could return it to the family, I read it to myself.

"This is to certify that on the 9th day of October 1942, the rites of matrimony were legally solemnized between Roderick Gregory Akner and Nora Lynn Nasaw at the Elizabeth County Courthouse in Hardin County in the presence of George A. Tanner and Judith C. Mayhurst."

A chord of bewilderment struck me as my eyes locked on my father's name. The date, October 9th, and the city's name, Elizabethtown, didn't escape my notice either.

Gregory and I married on that day and in that city, fifty-three years from the year written, and my father was there as a witness. The resonance felt more significant than the commonality.

My hands shook as I gripped the frame, and I had to set it on the desk before I dropped and broke it. It took me a few deep breaths to gather my bearings, and I traced my father's name with my fingertips, tears welling in my eyes.

I wanted to call Gregory and show him what I found. Something stirred inside me that the contents of this desk were a part of him as well. I felt drawn to the shoebox and pulled it free from the drawer. I removed the lid and discovered two bundles of letters tied with twine. I lifted one from the box, and my heartbeat escalated as if I knew the secrets of their contents.

The APO address to Sgt. Roderick G. Akner of the 1st Calvary Division base in Italy was written by Nora Lynn Akner of Covington, Kentucky. The next bundle, addressed in reverse, told me everything I needed to know about the Akners. By the postmarks on the envelopes, I knew they were newlywed and very much in love.

I untied the bundle and began sifting through it when I heard a voice whisper with insistence, “Read this one.”

I looked around, wondering where the voice came from. One envelope slipped from the pile and landed at my feet. Setting the rest down, I leaned forward and picked it up.

The envelope had a piece torn away, and an old rust-colored stain covered the entirety of its backside. Recognizing it was blood; I felt somewhat uneasy about handling it. Despite my reservations, I pulled out the letter and was amazed that the dried blood barely marred the edges. The letter had a fragmented, misshapen appearance along one side as I unfolded it.

I looked at it in awe, and the handwritten words drew me into the past.

January 1st, 1944

My Dearest Roddy,

New Year's Eve celebration didn't feel worth celebrating without you. At midnight, I blew a kiss to the sky and wished for a shooting star to bring it to you. I miss you! How many holidays must we remain apart?

Valentine's Day is next, and I pray on Cupid's arrow that this letter will reach you in time. Even though we will not be together, I take happiness in knowing that we already belong to one another. You are mine, and I will always be yours.

With this letter, I send you my heart. Please carry it in your breast pocket above your heart on February 14th, and I will do my best to keep you safe with all my prayers.

Love,

Nora

Mystified by the attachment I felt, I held the letter to my chest. Closing my eyes, I took a deep breath.

"You found it!" His voice came like that of a familiar old friend. I turned and looked up at a pair of striking blue eyes!

"Roderick?" My mouth dropped open like on a loose hinge. I realized I knew him as the memories came rushing back. He looked older than I remembered, with the addition of a few laugh lines and a touch of grey in his temples.

"Hello, Rachael." Roderick smiled, and those lines creased with distinction. He motioned to the letter I held. "I saved it before my blood saturated it."

"This letter? You had it in your pocket the day you were shot? How did everything get left inside a desk I bought?" I asked.

"Yes, as you requested, I put the letter in my pocket that day. And as far as everything inside the desk, you put it there. You said it was the safest place when we moved out of the apartment above the bar."

"I did?" I looked around the unfamiliar room, not knowing how I got there.

"You did." Roderick pointed at a mirror on the wall, and I saw Nora's reflection staring back in awe. *Nora!* The soul we shared. Another life. I realized I was back in her body again.

I shook my head and allowed the shock to subside before saying, "I guess I forgot. I've forgotten a lot of things."

"I didn't." Roderick smiled. "How's life treating you, Rachael? Did you take my advice to heart?"

"I did," my voice rasped. My legs felt wobbly as I stood, and my lips trembled.

"Good. It's good to see you again." Roderick hugged me, and my tears soaked into his shoulder. He held me for a long moment swaying back and forth like music was playing in the background.

"I thought it was a dream," I said. "It, it happened?"

"Nora remembers. She told me after you left, she was there throughout our shared experience. She said she was also there with you when you were a child. Your mother used to say you were talking with your guardian angel. Then one day…."

"She was gone," I concluded.

Roderick nodded. "There comes a time when we're made to let go and forget. When Nora died, and you were born, the transition did not sever the line between the first life to the next. Your consciousness was there, but Nora stayed with you for a time. She said your mother was very young and had a lot on her plate. And considering she was married to George," Roderick laughed, "It is fair to say I feel a great deal of sympathy for your mother."

I smiled, knowing Roderick was only joking. But I knew my father was sometimes demanding, and my mother's life wasn't easy. "Did you meet my mother?"

"No. I departed a few years before she and your father met."

"Was it somewhat the same with you and Gregory?" I asked. "He used to tell me he felt he was born in the wrong era?"

"Gregory was born with an innate sense of duty which may have been due to my life experience resonating within our soul. But it wasn't the same as with Nora and you."

I nodded. "How do you know all of this? You know when you'll die?"

"Nora has the gift of foresight. It comes and goes."

"You're not afraid?" I asked.

Roderick laughed. "Afraid of what? Nora and I have made a beautiful life together, just like you and Gregory have and will continue to do. We have a son named Benjamin Jacob and a daughter, Sarah Olivia. Our lives may be short, but we're making each day count. Nora is excited that we get to do it all over again. She's just a little disappointed that we'll have to wait till Gregory is thirty and you are nineteen. She told me to remind you to pray to God for me."

"I did. I prayed for you. I felt so alone without you."

"Me too." Roderick took hold of my face and kissed me on the lips. "Is it different?" he asked.

"A little." I smiled. "You're taller than Gregory, and Nora's shorter than me," I joked.

Roderick grinned. "Aside from the height difference."

"Oh!" I laughed as if I didn't know what he was referencing. But I knew! "I feel your love for Nora, and I can feel her love for you. It's different because of our bodies and the same because of our souls."

"I get it," he said. "Would you like to join me for a cup of coffee?"

"I don't drink coffee."

"What? You love coffee!"

"Nora loves coffee. I'm more of a tea drinker."

"But you drank coffee that day you spent with George and me," Roderick insisted.

"I did a few things I don't normally do that day."

"Like what?" he asked.

"For one, I don't dance. I'm a terrible dancer."

"Take a turn with me. For old times' sake," Roderick pleaded.

"I don't know how I was able to do it then." I looked at Nora's body. She had put on a little weight around her midsection, most likely from motherhood, but she still felt strong.

"Nora?" Roderick called.

I'm here; her voice rang richly in my ears. ***Remember me?*** she asked.

My eyes popped with amazement. "Oh, my go-oh-osh! I do!"

Nora's laughter followed the shock in my voice. My hands, our hands lifted, and Roderick took hold and placed them on his shoulders. Then he began to sing and step in time with the familiar words to a song that meant more to me now than before.

"You've gotta ac-cent-u-ate the positive
E-lim-i-nate the negative
And latch on to the affirmative
Don't mess with Mr. In-between."

Nora guided our feet as we kept in step with Roderick, and he continued to sing the rest of the song. The joy that bubbled within me had me chuckling as I sang along.

As the song ended, Roderick gave me a spin and pulled me in for a kiss on my cheek. Roderick took my hand and led me to sit in the chair I had arrived in. He took hold of Nora's written letter and placed it back in my hands.

I looked at the dried blood and torn edge. "Nora. She must have known. She, her letter saved your life! Literally!" A few of my tears broke upon the surface of the letter where the dried blood absorbed them. And I moved it so I wouldn't further damage an artifact so fragile and rare. Yet, it had defied a bullet. It defied death. And it made its way to me through time.

Roderick touched the letter and said, "If I had died that day, I would have seen to it that Nora never got that letter back. I wouldn't have made it to Heaven knowing she or you lost your faith because of it. Remember what I told you on our last day together, Rachael?"

A tear slipped from my eye, and I nodded. "All of it. I have faced crossroads in my life. Through everything, I recalled your words, 'Love is the victor in all battles! It will always lead us home,' and I've made it, Roderick. My love for you, Nora, Gregory, our children, and myself is *home*. I not only dwell there. It is the place in which I live."

I closed my eyes when Roderick leaned forward, kissed my forehead, and he said, "Then when my time comes, I can die a happy man knowing you've made it."

His voice became an echo like a memory.

SIERRA

Gregory's hand was on my shoulder, shaking me awake. The box of letters had fallen to the floor between my feet. I mumbled something, and Gregory shook me again. "Rachael! It's hot out here. You look like you passed out. Come inside."

I opened my eyes and was back in the present, still holding the letter to my chest. I lifted my head off my arm on the desk and leaned forward to grab the box. Gregory stopped me. "I'll get it. Just come inside. I'll bring it to you."

He helped me stand, and I swayed on my feet.

"Easy, wife! No shower diving!"

"I'm not in the shower," I grumbled.

"Same rules apply. Come on, woman. Inside." Gregor led me into the air conditioning, and I sat on the couch. He got me a glass of iced water, then made sure I took a drink before he took it from me and set it on the end table.

“There was a frame on the desk and a book,” I informed him.

“I’ll get it! Don’t get your panties in a bunch.” Gregory admonished.

“I’m not!” I protested.

“One of these days, woman! You’ll give me a heart attack with your fainting spells.”

I pointed my finger at him. “Don’t you dare!”

Gregory puffed out his chest. “Yeah? What are you going to do about it if I do?”

I laughed. “Do you realize how ridiculous you sound?”

“It’s my prerogative to be as ridiculous as I want. I earned it!”

“I would say so,” I agreed.

“What does that mean?” he challenged.

I threw my hands in the air. “Does it have to mean anything? Just scoot! Scoot that cute toosh out there and get those letters!”

Gregory opened the door and paused when I said, “And the frame! And the book!”

He huffed, turned, glared at me, and asked, “Anything else?”

“That’s all!” I shrugged my shoulders. Gregory muttered under his breath in comical belligerence, and I rolled my eyes as he closed the door behind him.

My husband! What could I say? I loved him despite his grumbly bear-like tendencies.

Sarah entered the living room and asked, “Are you and Dad throwing hands again?”

All three of our children were still living at home. Sarah worked part-time and attended online classes. Olivia helped care for the household pets and worked on her art projects. Finding work outside the house with her severe anxiety was challenging. Ben worked part-time, but with his disability, he didn't get many hours. Despite our challenges, we pulled together as a family and managed.

"Of course!" I replied. "A day wouldn't go by without your father disgruntled over one silly little thing or another."

"Where did he go?" she asked.

"Out to the garage. He's bringing me some letters."

"Letters? From who?"

"They were in the desk we bought at the estate sale."

Sarah opened the door to the garage. "Papa!" she yelled, "What are you doing?"

"Getting some things for your mother!" He hollered back.

Sarah stepped out, leaving the door open.

"Do you pay the electric bill? Close the door!" He yelled.

Sarah continued challenging Gregory as she closed the door, and I smiled. I always enjoyed their banter. It reminded me of two other people whose identities were at the tip of my brain. Since having woken from my second trip to visit the past, I realized those people were Roderick and my father, George. And for the first time, it made me wonder how much of my father's personality was in Sarah.

Genetics and ancestry are remarkable. God does this neat little thing where He recycles the best qualities of our character. Sometimes it's a snarky attitude.

Case in point, Sarah!

God plays up our best qualities. And from time to time, He recreates, out of love for what he sees, in our likenesses—case in point, my youngest sister's son, who looked so much like our father, we thought he was his clone.

It was uncanny.

Also, many subjects in museum portraits painted in different centuries hold striking resemblances to people alive today. Quite often, the eyes were the most striking similarity. The saying, 'The eyes are the windows to the soul,' spoke volumes in those accounts.

Something Roderick said reminded me of a scripture I'd read before. He told me to love myself as God does because I am 'fearfully and wonderfully made.'

Psalm 139:13-16 NIV

"For you created my inmost being; you knit me together in my mother's womb. I praise you because I am fearfully and wonderfully made; your works are wonderful, I know that full well. My frame was not hidden from you when I was made in the secret place when I was woven together in the depths of the earth. Your eyes saw my unformed body; all the days ordained for me were written in your book before one of them came to be."

'Fearfully and wonderfully made.' **We all are!**

It took me a time or two through the rinse, spin, and repeat cycles to finally get it.

VICTOR

I spent some time sifting through the letters. I read a few of them and shared them with Gregory. Being the World War II fanatic he was, he began categorizing and archiving them into his already ever-increasing collection of memorabilia. We needed a room spacious enough to accommodate these historical artifacts. We were growing a museum.

As we went through Roderick's and Nora's history, we reflected on ours. I told Gregory about my experience meeting Roderick while I was in Nora's body. He didn't call me crazy. He said my mind was an imaginarium, and it sounded like I had an out-of-body experience in my coma.

Gregory scarcely left my side when I was in the hospital. He cared for and checked on me diligently, and I knew how worried he was. It stole a piece of our lives together, but I recovered from that fall.

It was a hard-knock lesson learned. We added it to the many others journaled throughout the years. Because even when you're with your soul mate, it doesn't mean life is always smooth sailing.

On September 11th, 2001, the Twin Towers' fall, among other travesties, was a bitter tragedy. Violence born of hatred for our country took so many lives that day. That hatred stemmed from a distorted ideology in which self-appointed terrorists lined up to claim false crowns of martyrdom.

Subsequently, our twin girls came into the world on *9/11/2006.* They were the *11th* set of twins born within *two* months at the hospital where I gave birth, weighing *6lbs 11oz* and *5lbs 11oz*, respectively. The similarities within the numbers served as a reminder that positive things still come out of the negative, and God's timing is good.

Gregory was a soldier through and through, and he could handle an M16A2 with steady confidence. But as a dad, he held our girls, one in each arm, and walked with them shakily to the neonatal care unit. He expressed how frightened he was that he might fall or drop them.

He never faltered.

Gregory soldiered on as a wonderful father and helpmate.

When our family was young, Gregory and I remained on the fence about returning to Kentucky, where most of our family lived. We decided to stay in Texas, plant roots, and let our family grow. We'd found a church where we drew closer to God than we'd ever been before in our lives.

Throughout the years, one of my regrets was not visiting our family more often. Because time flew and before we knew it, our children were full-grown young adults who didn't really know their extended family too well. It was something that constantly gnawed at me.

Within four years, Gregory lost his parents, and I lost my mother. The pain was so deep and unbearable that I shut myself away and let the grief consume me to the point that I'd given up on living.

I ate, slept, and wrote a fiction book about a family separated by space and time but reunited in another world. The young girl had to find her strength and accept her fate to rise against the darkness that tried to consume the souls of those she loved. Through her love and the aid of those who loved her, she was triumphant in defeating the enemy. She was a representation of me and what I strived to be.

The irony was that, in reality, I pushed Gregory away, the very man who stayed by my side through thick and thin and back again. It broke me even more that I was this way. My inner turmoil placed me at odds against doing anything to make me feel worthy of his love, and it sent me into a downward spiral where I dug deeper and deeper, hoping to make the final break to the other side. I longed to see the light of day again, where the sun could shine on a happier tomorrow.

Gregory deserved better. And some days, I wished he would go and find it. Most of the time, I was scared that he *would* leave. Our children, as beautiful inside and out as they were, were challenged with Autism, ADHD, anxiety, and depression. I couldn't help thinking their disabilities were my fault, and I felt useless to carry the weight alone.

I needed him. With all my taking, the less I had to give. I felt so selfish. Gregory looked tired and older than he should have, but he never gave up on showing his love. He still desired a physical connectedness, which I could not reciprocate. I wanted to, but the brutal anguish had created a wall, a stronghold in my mind that I could not break through. I would look at the state of my body and think so low of myself. I struggled with intimacy and declined his initiations more and more often.

I had fallen asleep a time too many until the day I fell completely. I thought it was too late. Then my soul made a journey, and I saw that it was still possible to break through the darkness. It was a lesson I had to learn. If there were still a fighting chance, I would finally take it.

***

The circle of time through the past and present created a cornerstone of faith, setting a place for something miraculous to happen in my life. I had stood at a crossroads where I allowed fear to hold me captive. My fear, born of pride, had nearly ended my life. I was complacent and too proud to ask for help. I was sinking and drowning in a sea of grief.

My father had died from a ruptured vessel. Patched together after his accident five years prior, he had lived and loved with the courage and conviction in his heart and stayed as long as possible in this world.

To see and experience Gregory and myself as Roderick and Nora was a life-altering and healing experience I would never forget. In my faltering and misgiving, I'd allowed fear to take hold. It was a wake-up call at this stage of my life. Gregory and I were getting older, but we still had more time to live.

The words I wrote took on a new meaning. It was no longer a futile attempt to appease the trends of the masses. Whether or not I became a successful author no longer mattered. I wrote because it was in my nature to do so. My words mattered within the depths of my heart as I looked more to God to fill the emptiness inside and become more of what His will required. I did so of my free will, making me feel less tethered to the pride that bound me to fear.

I still struggled from time to time. But the knot had loosened enough that I tied those lines of fate to an anchor of faith. And most days, I felt the freedom to float. On those solemn days that threatened to pull me down, I called on Jesus to cast the nets and fish me from the waves too powerful to fight with my strength alone.

And one night, I heard his voice. "Don't you dare give up, Rachael!" Roderick's voice echoed in my sleep.

I squeezed my eyelids, trying to bring enough moisture to open them. I looked at my laptop on my bedside table, where I had begun writing our story. Gregory lay on his side of the bed to my right, moaning in his sleep. He did this every so often. He denied having PTSD, but it sounded like he had the kind of nightmares one would associate with it.

I reached over and rubbed his chest, and he stirred awake. He snorted, and his hand touched mine, reassuring me he was okay.

"You were having a nightmare," I said.

"Was I?" he asked.

"You don't remember?"

"No." He patted my hand again and settled back into a gentler sleep.

He rarely remembered his dreams, yet his inner soldier still fought the battles of his past. Something hadn't occurred to me before. Having seen Roderick's chest wound, I realized Gregory often placed his hand in the same spot when he had occasional muscle spasms.

Gregory, too, had faced many battles and crossroads in his life. Still, he fought with the courage of his convictions, never against them. I always admired him for it. My husband's body was tired and battle weary. He griped and grumbled occasionally but never faltered in faithfulness and love for me, his family, and God. He was my soulmate. And I would follow him to our next destination.

ROMEO

The phone was ringing from its hook in the kitchen. I opened my eyes, staring at the ceiling for a moment. I yawned, stretched, rolled, and fell out of bed. I was stunned as I took in the familiarity of my bedroom. But it was the bedroom in my mother and stepfather's house. My sister's twin bed sat against the perpendicular wall, but she wasn't in it.

"Rachael," my mother's voice called. The bedroom door opened, and my heart froze when I saw her.

"MOM?" I cried. I didn't know why the sight of her made me feel so many emotions. Shock, sadness, dismay, and overwhelming joy had me reeling.

She came to me. "What's wrong?"

I grabbed at the bed, fumbling as I lifted my body. As my mother came closer, I stumbled backward, and with a springing flop, my butt bounced on the bed. She sat with me, and I instantaneously threw my arms around her and cried. It was like I'd lost her and hadn't seen her in years.

I couldn't let her go, and as I continued to sob, I said, "I fell."

She chuckled as she patted and rubbed my back in soothing circles. "Oh, my poor baby. Are you hurt?"

"No!" I cried more.

"What is it?" She took my arms and held me away to see my face. She brushed my bangs aside and looked at me with beautiful green eyes.

She was young and healthy, in her late thirties, with her lovely rosy complexion and light brown hair with highlights cut to style the way she wore it that time of her life—that time in my life when I was in my late teens.

Nineteen, I thought. I wondered how this could be. How was my mother here now? I felt like there was somewhere I was supposed to go on this day.

"Oh!" my mother said as if remembering something important. She looked at me sadly and said, "It was your father's birthday two days ago. He would've been."

"Sixty-seven years old," I said.

She nodded as her eyes glistened. "I miss your daddy too. But you know he'd want us to keep living our lives and be happy."

She held me, stroking my hair, and I felt safe and cherished in her arms. A colossal piece that felt like it had been missing fell into place, but there was still something else I couldn't find a reason to.

"Marissa just called," she told me. "She asked if you would still meet up with her after she got off work. I told her you were sleeping, but I'd tell you to call her back."

Instantly, I stopped crying, and I felt like this day had some other purpose. It wasn't just hanging out with my best friend and, more than likely, her boyfriend, Johnathan. There was some underlying feeling that seemed to tug at my inner being.

And as much as I wanted to stay the entire day with my mom, I knew I had to go at some point. I spent the whole morning talking with her, watching her put her hair in hot rollers, select an outfit, get dressed, style her hair, and put on her makeup. It was part of her daily routine.

My mother loved her jewelry. She dug around in her tall jewelry armoire, picking through her vast selection and showing me her latest buys. After many years of sacrifice and caring for everyone, her nursing career finally afforded her to buy some nice things for herself.

She asked me which necklace, bracelet, or earrings she should wear. She completed her look for the day and finished off by spraying the light fragrance of Jovonne Musk on her neck. She motioned for me to lift my chin and gave a spritz of it to me.

In the kitchen, she pulled out meats, cheeses, veggies, and bread, and we made monster-sized sandwiches. After years of feeding my sisters and me, she was still in the habit of feeding a small army. She cut the sandwiches into smaller portions and wrapped and refrigerated what she would take to work through the week.

It didn't matter what we talked about; I felt love, warmth, kindness, and consideration whenever I spoke with her. Talking to my mother was the next best thing to communicating with God. He'd imbued my mother with the essence of a lifting spirit. Her simple words held wisdom and healing as she expressed herself in a way that never felt condescending.

My mother had a hard life and suffered tremendous heartache. Still, she had overcome so many battles and soldiered on. She was my hero in so many ways.

"What are your plans with Marissa tonight?" she asked.

My plans? It didn't feel like *my* plans.

"I'm not sure. I guess we're going to eat and hang out."

"Be careful out there." She stood and hugged me. My emotions welled again, not wanting to let her go, but the pull to go out the door was becoming more urgent like I would miss some divine appointment if I didn't leave soon.

As if knowing it, my mother pushed my hair away from the sides of my face, cupping my cheeks in her soft hands; she looked into my eyes. "I am so proud of you. You have accomplished so much. I know God has wonderful plans for your life. You hang in there, my tender-hearted girl. Life gets hard from time to time, but lean on God's strength, and He will pull you through."

My eyes watered. "I'm so happy I got to spend the day with you. I love you, mama."

She kissed my cheeks and smiled. "I love you too, Rachael."

I didn't know why, but this moment felt like a heart-wrenching goodbye. I hesitated to leave, to let my mother go. But then she told me, "Go! Have a good time. I'll see you soon."

I hugged her tightly and kissed her cheek. "I'll see you soon."

Then I walked to the door, opened it, looked back at her for what felt like the last time, then turned and closed it.

***

I stood at the counter talking to Marissa as she finished her shift at the 'Taco Smell' we so jokingly called the fast food restaurant. Her boyfriend, Johnathan, worked with her cleaning, sweeping the floors.

"Johnathan's brother is in town. He wants to take us all out for dinner and a moving," Marissa said.

His brother? I wondered to myself, *Why would he want to take us anywhere?"*

I'd never heard Johnathan or Marissa mention any brother other than Warren, who was thirteen years older than Johnathan and married.

I spent the last four years third-wheeling it, occasionally going out with Marissa and Johnathan. Marissa and I met in high school during our first year when I was new and didn't know anybody. She was the first person kind enough to speak to me. It was as if she knew how timid I was and offered an olive branch that would soon bloom into a glorious friendship. She was a kindred spirit, kind, intelligent, beautiful, and popular.

She and Johnathan didn't start dating till our sophomore year. And since Marissa and I were so tight-knit, Johnathan didn't complain about my presence. The three of us got along pretty well. We had similar interests, and I did have a few other good friends I went out with, so they had time alone.

Marissa tried to help me find a boyfriend, but none of them sparked my interest, and the boys I did crush on weren't wholly interested in me. It didn't matter. They each had their ways about them that were off-putting in one way or another. I couldn't establish a real connection, one worth taking a risk with my heart.

My mother was right; my heart was always tender. It wouldn't only break but pulverize like someone took a tenderizing mallet and beat it to a pulp, and the pain might be too much to come back from. So I pushed a few likable suitors away. They were friendly but not long-term boyfriend material. I didn't want to attach myself to anyone at that point anyway. I'd witnessed the ups and downs my other friends had been through, and I wanted to be sure I'd found someone special before I invested my heart.

Marissa and Johnathan clocked out as I waited for them in the lobby. "He's here." Johnathan pointed out the window, and we all went outside and watched from the sidewalk as a sporty red car pulled into a parking spot three spaces down from where we stood.

A young man exited the vehicle, and I was immediately struck by his dark hair and blue eyes. Seeing his eyes felt like a miraculous answer to a prayer I had prayed some time ago. He looked older, somewhere in his mid to late twenties. His hair, cut short and styled neatly, didn't look like the typical shaggy heads I was used to seeing around town. I thought his nose was a tad prominent, like my own. And he had a full, neatly trimmed dark mustache which looked too mature on his youthful face.

"Hey there, little brother!" He smiled and greeted Johnathan. He looked at Marissa, saying hello to her, and then he looked at me. Something inside of me akin to a spark of recognition flickered to life. It was hard to explain the feeling, but as I looked at him and he smiled, I felt drawn to him, like his soul was the answer to what was missing inside of me.

"Hi, I'm Rachael," I said with a shy timidity.

He held me with his blue eyes, and I saw the light, the heat in his stare. It was raw, unbridled attraction and much more. I saw the offer of a partnership and a future. When he offered his hand to shake, and we touched, it felt like we weren't meeting for the first time but reconnecting.

My heartbeat escalated when he looked at me with surety and said,

"Nice to meet you, Rachael. I'm Gregory."

And hearing his name was an end to my loneliness, a balm to my brokenness, and the spark that set my soul aflame. So began a whirlwind romance with all the delights, harmony, and joy which made two souls reunite at the crossroads. They stood hand in hand and started their journey HOME.

NORA'S DIARY

July 26, 1964

Dear Rachael,

My heart quivered when I saw his name in the newspaper. Gregory Samuel Talbert was born yesterday to Sarah and Benjamin Talbert. He was one month early, weighing 4lbs, 5 oz, but I knew he would leave the hospital in a week safe and healthy. I smiled to myself as I read the paper. Then folding it, I waved at the heat and felt relief knowing he'd arrived. I felt an acute ache when I thought of how long I'd have to wait till we met again. But then I looked up and saw a young girl walking alone. She sat on a swing, and I felt drawn to her. I told her my name, and she told me hers.

Olivia.

Long dark hair and beautiful green eyes smiled back at me. I instantly knew who Olivia was and kindly told her it wasn't safe to play at the park alone. She said she felt safe there. I asked her why, and Olivia looked down, dragging the toes of her shoes in the dirt. She looked at me and asked if there were any nice dads in the world.

I told her about our Roderick, and with a glimmer of hope in her eyes, Olivia thanked me. I offered a hug, and she accepted. I felt the connection between us. Olivia was a kindred spirit, tender and loving despite her circumstances. She looked at me with a question in her eyes. One that, deep down, I believed she knew the answer to.

I asked her if she was okay, but she told me she couldn't talk about it. Then I knew why she said she felt safe at the park. I recalled when you told Roderick that your mother's childhood was hard. Olivia talked about her brothers and sisters and how much she loved them—especially her sister April who looked out for her most.

She said April would return soon after checking on their mother and making sure their daddy had left before going home.

My heart went out to her, and I asked if I could speak with her mother to offer a safe place to stay with Benjamin, Sarah, and me. I wouldn't mind the extra company since Roderick had passed away eight months ago.

Olivia told me it was all right; her mother knew a kind person willing to help.

I asked the friend's name, and she told me, George.

Olivia smiled when I told her I had a friend named George, who was a good man. George had faced a crossroad that took him in a direction away from our lives. I didn't fault him and knew it had to be. He did write off and on from whatever location the life as a carnival worker took him. Sometime later, I heard he had resettled in Cincinnati. He attended Roderick's funeral, and it hit him so hard. He offered to help, but I let him know we were well provided for. After that, I heard from him less and less. I didn't hear his name again until today. I believe the Lord is preparing George for what's to come. And I know He is preparing Olivia as well.

I gave Olivia a talk. I told her she would face many difficult trials in her life. And sometimes, she may think she lost the battle, but she should never give up. Good will come. It was the same as Roderick told you. Time and pressure make diamonds. Olivia would face tremendous pressure in her future, but she would come out of it as a diamond.

With great hesitance, I let her go when her sister April arrived. I watched them till they disappeared around a corner and accepted that I might never see her again in this life. But I would see her in my next. And I will be there in one way or another for as long as possible to help you, Rachael.

Take care of yourself. For me, Roderick, Gregory, and our family.

Love Always,

Nora

NEVER THE END

Through the eyes of each window
Through each shade of color, we see
Each life, from past to present
A soul abides in thee

I see yours,
And you see mine
From present to past
Through the crevasse of time

As we step through the trenches
Both forward and back
Quivering hearts press onward
Navigating Faith’s cross paths

We bear through the trials
With the love that we share
And never lose hope
As long as together, we are there

GREETINGS FROM THE AUTHOR

Thank you for reading Crossroads Soulmates. I hope you enjoyed Rachael's story. This book is my fifth work of fiction and first romance novella. Part of Rachael's story is very personal, as it touches upon truths of my struggles with depression, including accounts of my journey through the crossroads. I thank God for my husband, life partner, and soulmate. His support throughout our twenty-eight years of marriage has meant so much to me. I appreciate him for soldiering through all our crazy ups and downs together.

I want to thank the men and women in uniform who have served our country with courage, conviction, and dignity. Your sacrifice allows the many freedoms we treasure. With my sincerest gratitude, I tip my pen and salute you.

If you're struggling with depression, know that you're not alone. My thoughts and prayers are with you as we journey forward together. I know it's hard to see the light at the end of the tunnel. Pray and seek help from God and those around you.

Each day is a new blessing and a possible breakthrough. Every breath is a blessing to fill your lungs and release what needs letting go. 'Give it all to God, for he cares for you. You are fearfully and wonderfully made and have a future and purpose.'

Never give up!

OTHER TITLES BY THIS AUTHOR

Young Adult Supernatural Romance
Generation Stone Revelation Light Calling
https://www.amazon.com/Generation-Stone-Revelation-Light-Calling-ebook/dp/B096PY2R8W

+Adult Paranormal Romance+
Dark Trespass Series
A Necromancer's Heart
Book One
https://www.amazon.com/Dark-Trespass-Book-One-Necromancers-ebook/dp/B0BGVPQRKS/
A Necromancer's Peril
Book Two
https://www.amazon.com/gp/product/B0BGXT5PW8
A Necromancer's Fight
Book Three
https://www.amazon.com/gp/product/B0BGW2WX3V

Poetry w/illustration
Ghost Written Enda Grave
https://www.amazon.com/Ghost-Written-Enda-Grave-ebook/dp/B0BK59KMXM

www.ingramcontent.com/pod-product-compliance
Lightning Source LLC
LaVergne TN
LVHW020637100826
845148LV00012B/2212

* 9 7 8 1 7 3 7 3 2 4 9 7 3 *